A Beautiful Mess

By: Emily McKee

A Beautiful Mess

Limitless Publishing, LLC
Kailua, HI 96734
www.limitlesspublishing.com

Formatting: Limitless Publishing

ISBN-13: 978-1495218002
ISBN-10: 1495218007

Dedication

Erica

I am so grateful to have met you. I wouldn't have started writing novels if it weren't for you. I'm so thankful for your friendship and help through this process. You will forever be in my heart.

"This life is what you make it. No matter what, you're going to mess up sometimes, it's a universal truth. But the good part is you get to decide how you're going to mess it up."

— Marilyn Monroe

Prologue

2 years earlier

Ashlynn

Singing along to my favorite Sarah McLachlan song, "Fallen," I thought about the lyrics. I have never messed up so much that I've met the bottom. I've never messed up before. I started to get lost in my own thoughts when the song stopped playing, mid line. My eyes widened and I looked over to Dad.

His hand was moving away from the power button on the radio.

I waved my hand in the air. "Dad! Do you not know that "Fallen" by Sarah McLachlan is like the BEST song ever?"

I was just getting ready to turn the radio back on to sing along to my all-time jam but Dad slapped my hand away. He just shrugged his shoulders and kept his eyes on the road while I was going off on my little rant.

1

"I'm sorry, honey but I wanted to talk to you about something before we got to school. You mind giving your old dad a few minutes?"

Dad and I were on our way to the University of Maryland for the beginning of my four years of college. I was so excited and I couldn't wait to meet new people.

Try new things.

Experience life and everything it had to offer.

Turning to him, I saw that he was looking at me and I gave him this, *Seriously? Yeah, because we won't talk every day on the phone and Skype once a week* look.

Letting out a breath, he poked his lower lip out and said in this funny and pathetic voice, "After all, you aren't going to see your dad till probably Thanksgiving, baby girl."

I just laughed at his pathetic, yet lovable, excuse but then I looked at him seriously because I wanted to remember him this way. When he was joking around with me and acting like a little kid. When he would terrorize me and joke around about it. When we were talking and laughing with one another because I would miss him terribly after he dropped me off at school and I was all by myself. I wanted to make him proud and not make a mess of things.

Daddy never went to college and said that he always regretted not going. I joked around and said it was because he didn't get to go to all of college parties. He would always laugh and say, "Yeah, you caught me."

Dad was a bad boy in high school and then his senior year fell in love with mom. Mom was a bookworm like myself who fell in love with Dad the first time she saw him on his motorcycle. After high school, Dad decided to work. While he was smart, he couldn't stand sitting in a classroom and listening to a teacher lecture on and on about math or science. History or English. It was kind of ironic, actually, because he lectured me all of the time growing up.

Choosing the right friends.

Choosing the wrong friends.

Being too nice to people.

Being too mean to people and so on and so forth.

Of course we would joke around for a few minutes and then somehow we would get on the topic of Mom and Dad. He told me stories about how fast he fell in love with Mom. I always loved his lectures because then I could hear stories about Mom. Of course Dad told me stories about Mom to keep her memory with us, but I loved when he told me the stories about first seeing her because I knew that love existed because of them. I was the product of two people in love.

Tearing up from the stories of Mom, he would then get all serious and say, "But I do really regret not going to college. My Annette, your mom, went to college, and at times I felt terrible because I wanted to be able to provide for us in a way that I was proud of. I wanted to spoil you and your mom rotten and give you both the world. Your mom would always say that the only thing she needed in her life was me because I was the world. And then when we had you she said, 'The only things I need in my life are the love of my life and our little sunshine we made together.'"

Mom always referred to me as her little sunshine and would always sing, "You Are My Sunshine, My Only Sunshine" to me when I was little. She and Dad had trouble getting pregnant and decided to give up. They were happy with one another but they wanted desperately to have children. She decided to call me her little sunshine because she said I brought light to the world, referring to her world with Dad.

Breaking me from my thoughts, Dad said, "So I want you to go to college. I want you to have fun, but I also want you to make something of yourself and be happy with your choices, and don't mess up too much."

He then turned to me with this serious look and I kind of, sort of, had an idea about what my dad wanted to change the topic to, so I took a few deep breaths and said, "Okay, what now, Daddy?"

I thought by calling him daddy, he would get tears in his eyes and forget all about where he was taking this conversation, but no such luck. I decided to turn and look out the window because I was so embarrassed.

He began to stutter and kept clearing his throat, so I knew he was embarrassed about having to talk to me about *this*. This being, "I wanted to talk to you about being safe. And by being safe, I mean with boys—"

I was about to yell at him to just stop because I would have rather stabbed myself in my nether regions with a rusty knife than hear my dad talk to me about boys and sex. I mean, he wasn't actually talking about sex, but I knew that was what he was referring to. Plus he tried to have the sex talk with me once and that experience just didn't work out very well. I have mentally blocked the experience out of my noggin for the rest of my life. He referred to it as the birds and the bees, which I still don't understand! Not the act, but why it's called the birds and the bees. That just doesn't make sense to me.

He turned to me at the next red light and said, "… but I love you, honey and we're all each other has. I just want you to think with your head and not with your heart. I'm just so proud of you and I don't want to see you get hurt. There are good guys and then there are bad guys. I know you're smart, so you'll figure out which is which."

Dad paused so I could let his words seep in.

I knew the differences between good guys and bad guys. Okay, what I mean to say is that I knew of them. I didn't really get to experience all of what high school had to offer. Of course I went to my classes and did the afterschool activities like soccer and chorus.

But I didn't get to experience the house parties and the sneaking out of your bedroom in the middle of the night to do absolutely nothing but feel like you're accomplishing everything. To feel like you're messing up in the best way possible because you're living. You're making mistakes and you're learning from them.

I was friends with everybody in high school and I was asked out on dates, but there just wasn't that thing. That spark. Where you feel the fireworks and your heart skips a beat. Where all you do is think about that person; in a non-stalkerish way, of course.

Where you talk all of the time about absolutely nothing but you feel like you're connecting on a certain level with the person. Where you understand one another and for once you're selfless because you think about what the other person needs before yourself.

I'm a smart girl when it comes to education. Taking tests and doing homework. Staying up at all hours of the night to do projects and write papers. But when it comes to relationships I fucking suck at it, which is probably the biggest understatement of the year.

Decade.

Century.

Millennium.

My problem is not finding a guy but actually feeling something for them. A lot of people say that I'm picky, but I don't want to waste my time. Wasting my time on someone when I know from the beginning when I first shake their hand or look into their eyes that it won't last.

We won't last.

Life is too short to waste your time, so I'm not. It's a smart thing, but it's also the dumbest thing because my life is quickly passing me by and before I know it I'm going to be on my death bed. So while my dad is talking about the good versus the bad and the right versus wrongs in life I'm thinking about finally starting mine.

Going to college parties.

Getting drunk and then suffering from the horrible hangovers.

Wearing sweats and ratty t-shirts to class.

Messing around and enjoying it.

We have long since moved on from that red light and have now pulled into the parking lot of the school. Kids are moving in and parents are hugging their kids and I'm instantly nervous. My palms began to sweat and my heart plummeted and before I knew it I was freaking out. I had never been away from home for an extended period of time.

I guess part of it was because my mom died in a car accident when I was four. It was just any normal day where she was running errands and picking up groceries. And then my dad got a call from the police saying his wife, my mom, was gone.

Ever since then my dad and I have been really close. Of course there were some awkward times when Daddy had to teach me about periods. Buying me tampons and pads at the convenience store. He took me bra shopping and we argued about whether or not a bikini was skimpy or non-skimpy.

But there were also really good times. He took me prom dress shopping and cheered me on at all of the soccer games. I could pick his voice out over anybody else's at my chorus concerts. He took me to the movies to see chick flicks when he really wanted to see aliens and zombies attacking people. *Trust me, we saw plenty of those as well.* I've lived a pretty good life and I'm lucky.

Daddy must have heard me take a gasp of air because the next thing I knew, he was placing his hand over mine and squeezing. He was giving me reassurance and telling me everything was going to be okay.

Getting my suitcases out of the car, we started to walk into the building where I would be living for my freshman year. With shaky fingers, I got my key and swipe card from my Resident Advisor and then walked to the front door of room 312. I began to slide my key into the hole when the door opened and out walked this drop-dead gorgeous guy.

He was wearing cargo shorts with a green top that brought out the bluish-green color of his eyes. His blond hair was shaved and he had little bit of scruff on his face.

My jaw dropped open and my heart started to beat twice, maybe even three times as fast, but at the same time it felt like it had slowed down. I had always read in books or saw in movies the first time two people meet and they feel that instant connection. I'd always thought it was bullshit but also the most romantic thing I had ever seen. That instant connection with the sparks and fireworks. With the rapidly beating heart and the serenity you felt while you just stared at this person and probably acted like a total idiot and looked like a moron with a stupid look on your face.

Blinking a few times to make sure he wasn't just a figment of my imagination, I was brought back to reality and could see Daddy out of the corner of my eye, looking between the two of us and shaking his head back and forth. *Clearly, he wasn't pleased.* The cute guy put his hand out in front of me and started to say something when some girl nudged him out of the way and grabbed me in a hug.

My bags dropped to the floor and she started squealing and jumping up and down. She put her hands on my shoulders and pushed back and said, "I'm Jade. You must be Ashlynn?"

I began to laugh and said, "Well, if I wasn't then that would have been really awkward."

I heard somebody laughing and I turned to my left and noticed that it was the cute guy. I looked back at Jade for an answer.

Waving her hand around she said, "Oh, that's Jason, my twin brother. He'll be around a lot. I hope you don't mind."

I turned to him and I knew that my eyes were bugging out of my head. *Mind? Not in the slightest.*

He put his hand out again and said, "I'm Jason. It's nice to meet you, Ashlynn."

I put my hand out to shake his and the second our skin touched, I felt a jolt of electricity jump through me. *That ain't no spark, it's like being shocked back to life.*

I could tell he felt it too, but he quickly let go of my hand and turned to his sister. "So, I'll see you ladies later?"

Jade just nodded. "Yeah, be here around nine."

Jason nodded his head up and down and then turned to me. "I'll see you later, Ashlynn."

Oh you most certainly will. Instead lamely, I said, "Okay."

As soon as he left, Jade helped Daddy and I carry all of my bags in. After organizing my room and working through the hassle of getting the television plugged in and getting the damn internet to connect to my laptop, it was time for Daddy to leave.

Jade was sitting on her bed listening to music when I started to walk Daddy out. Before the door closed the entire way, Jade yelled, "Nice to meet you, Mr. Miller."

Daddy poked his head back in and said, "You too, Jade. Take care of my little girl."

I heard Jade giggling and then she said, "Oh, I most certainly will. Advil, Midol, and Tylenol are all in stock!"

Once the door closed, I put my hand in Daddy's and we walked back to his car in silence. I'd known I was going to be starting college four hours away but it wasn't actually hitting me until that moment.

We walked over to the driver's side and Daddy unlocked the car and opened the door. His back was to me and when he turned around, there were tears in his eyes and I instantly wrapped my arms around his waist and rested my head on his chest. He wrapped me in his arms as well, his head rested on top of mine. We stood like that for a while and then Daddy put me at arm's length. He wiped away his tears and said, "Ugh, something must have flown in my eye."

I just chuckled. "I love you, Daddy."

He continued wiping his eyes and sniffled. I wrapped my arms around him again and kissed him on the cheek. "Always."

He kissed me on the top of the head. "Well, you better get back in there. Just remember to have fun but be smart in your decisions."

I nodded my head and said, "I will."

He poked his lower lip out. That look said that he was in deep concentration and lost in his thoughts. He kissed me again on the cheek and then got into the car and started it up. I closed his door and started to walk backwards, waving to him.

He put his seatbelt on and then lowered his window. "Watch out for that boy, Ash. I can tell he's one of the bad ones and I don't want to clean up the mess afterwards." As soon as the words left his mouth, Daddy winked at me, backed out of the parking spot, and began to drive away.

I kept waving to him and then under my breath I said, "Don't I know it," and my, oh my, was I looking forward to getting to know that beautiful mess of a man.

Chapter 1

Jason

God, I need this vacation. Christy had been blowing up my phone all of the time, which is funny because she rarely ever blew me. Fuck, she wasn't even that good in bed. I hate it when I have to do all of the work and the girl just lays there like a fucking blow up doll.

Sometimes I wondered if a blow up doll would be better. That way I don't have to hear all of the fake ass whining and horrible moaning when it's not even needed. I've often wondered about just using my hand, but when I can get my cock in some girl's wet pussy, then I'd much rather do that.

Hey, I'm a guy, so don't judge me.

Ryder had organized this entire thing because he wanted to surprise Iz for her birthday. Plus we could do a huge party for Sarah and Gabe's upcoming nuptials. Since Ryder and Iz were already in Las Vegas for the tattoo convention, it was Sarah, Gabe,

Patrick, Jade, Ash, myself, and for some reason, Ash's douche bag ex, Derrick, tagging along for the party.

It's not that I didn't like Derrick, he seemed like a pretty cool dude, but since he and Ash broke up it just wasn't sitting right with me. Ash is like a sister to me and I'll protect her like I'd protect Jade. They're my top girls and I'd do anything for them.

When planning this trip, I knew Sarah and Gabe were going to room together. I knew Jade would need her own room ... for obvious reasons. I sure as fuck didn't want to room with Derrick because I would have probably beat the living shit out of him for breaking up with Ash and I knew Ash would have probably been uncomfortable rooming with Derrick, so I decided Ash and I should room together.

I gave her the lamest excuse ever, saying, "It would just be cheaper for us to room together. You know what I mean?" I felt like a total fuck-up but she just shrugged her shoulders like it didn't matter to her. It kind of hurt. No, scratch that; it hurt like a motherfucker. It felt like I was getting stabbed in the heart and she was twisting the knife inside me. But this is the way it should be because Ash doesn't need a mess like me in her life.

We've known each other since our freshman year of school but nothing would ever happen between us.

Ash is fucking gorgeous but I'm a mess. Mess is kind of an understatement, but it's the closest thing I can think of. Anyway, Ash doesn't need that in her life. She deserves someone who is ... well, not me.

I couldn't bear to see Ash hurt because of me because I know with so much certainty that I would fuck it up. Besides, Ash is way out of my league.

The girl is fucking incredible. She has these nice perky tits that are just begging to be sucked on. She has these plump, fuck-me lips and I want a taste. But I don't think a taste would do it for me because once I got a taste of just how sweet she was, I would probably never be the same.

Not only does she have an incredibly amazing body but she's fucking hilarious. She always has a witty comment and she's always laughing about something. I swear her laugh does me in. Every single time I hear it I feel alive. Her laugh is amazing, but I especially love it when I can get her to laugh. She holds her stomach and she laughs so hard that her tits bounce up and down.

Every single time she laughs like that I picture her riding my cock. I get hard just thinking about being in her tight, wet pussy, legs on either side of me, and her hair falling over her shoulders, but cold water instantly douses my hard on because while Ash has a fuck-me body, I know she's sweet and safe.

Throughout the years, I often wondered why she never dated anyone, but then all of a sudden this year she met Derrick and BAM, they were in a relationship. I figured since she was in one, I might as well start dating Christy.

Christy and I had fucked every once in a while. I had met her at a party and she was all over me. Of course I was drunk, and taking her home, that night I attempted to fuck Ash out of my system. After that, I guess you could say we were fuck buddies. Whenever I needed a release, she was there, lying on her back, wet and ready. I didn't care about getting her off. I just needed to fuck Ashlynn out of my head. But every time I looked at Christy, my dick would start to get soft. Any girl, for that matter, really. So I would close my eyes, and when I closed my eyes every single time I saw Ash. Before I knew it I would be pumping into Christy and coming. I always had to bite my lip because there were a few times when I almost roared Ashlynn's name.

I may be an asshole but I know calling another girl's name out in bed is, well, you just don't do it. I mean, unless your cock and balls aren't important to you. So I just picture the girl in my head while slamming into another girl and trying to block out the fake moans and whimpers because the only whimpers and moans I want to hear are Ash's.

The second I found out Ash broke up with Derrick, I quit *seeing* Christy. I just couldn't take it anymore. I thought maybe since Ashlynn was happy, I would be happy, but her happiness was not because of me. It was with a guy she barely knew and I hated every second of it. They were always so touchy feely around me and every single time I wanted to beat the fuck out of him. It was bad enough I had to see him hold her hand or kiss her on the lips, but I became enraged thinking about what they were doing behind closed doors, or when I wasn't there.

I also hated the little prick because when nobody else was looking he would give me these little winks or smiles. Almost as if he was baiting me and telling me that he was with Ashlynn and I wasn't and probably never would be.

I still held out a small amount of hope that maybe Ash could fix the huge ass problems in my life, but I knew it wouldn't be easy. And plain and simple, I honestly didn't think I was worth saving, so I let her live her life.

I sounded like a fucking stalker but she meant everything to me. I held out for the moments where I could make her laugh from a comment. I held out for the moments that I could hold her in my arms while she cried. I held out for the moments where I got to see her beautiful face and that smile she gave me. Sometimes I'd watch her when she smiled at other people and I swear to Christ the way she looked at me was different compared to everyone else. But I thought that my mind was just playing crazy tricks on me because Ash would never look in my direction. To her I was just her best friend's annoying twin brother and nothing else.

There have been numerous times where I had wanted to tell Ash how I felt about her or show her. I'd wanted to throw her up against the wall and just devour her mouth. Say, "fuck the world," and go for it, but she didn't need someone flipping it upside down, sideways, front to back, and every which way in between.

Although now that I mention that, it would be nice if we were naked up against the wall or in the backseat of a car fucking each other's brains out. But this is Ash and I wouldn't want to fuck her. I would want to take my time with her and have her moan and writhe in enjoyment and come undone beneath me. Over and over again.

***

I don't know what it was but ever since we got on the plane to come and surprise Iz for her birthday, something was just sticking out about Ashlynn and I couldn't take it much longer. The second I put my bag in the overhead compartment, she made little grunting noises of distaste and disgust. She didn't talk to me the entire flight to Vegas—she just put her ear buds in and listened to music while reading a book. Since I had no form of entertainment, I just slept and dreamt about Ash.

Once we all checked into our rooms and dropped off our bags, we went to go surprise Iz for her birthday. She was so excited when she opened the door, and after the initial shock, she let us all in. We hung out for a little bit and then Ryder sent Isabelle, Sarah, Jade, Patrick, and Ash to the spa for the day to get facials and a bunch of girly shit done to them.

Not one of them needed it, especially Ash. She was a lot like Iz in that she rarely wore makeup and when she did, it was mascara. Ash is a beautiful girl but I always wondered what it would be like seeing her wake up in the morning in my arms.

After the girls left, Ryder, Gabe, Derrick, and I went down to the casinos to do some gambling. None of us were really that good but we had fun drinking a few beers and bullshitting about nothing important. Ryder wouldn't shut up about how happy he was with Iz. Gabe couldn't shut up about how he couldn't wait to marry Sarah. Meanwhile, I wanted to punch both of them in their fucking faces because they just kept rambling.

I was happy they were both happy, but they just kept talking and talking and talking. So I just picked up my beer bottle and started chugging when Ryder said, "So, Derrick, what's going on with you?"

I wasn't really interested in hearing what that fuck had to say, so I tried to mentally block it out but then he said, "Oh, I'm dating someone."

I started choking on my beer and when I calmed down, I looked over at the asshole.

He was going on and on about how amazing the person was and how he saw a future with them.

I instantly saw red and started yelling at him. "Are you fucking serious? You just broke up with Ash! What the fuck is wrong with you? Why are you even here?"

I slammed my beer bottle on the table and was getting up to knock the bastard out when Ryder stepped behind me and said, "Calm down, Jason."

Somehow I managed to get him off me and turned my anger on him. "Are you kidding me right now! Why was that asshole even invited?"

That's when Gabe stood up and grabbed my arm. "Can I see you for a minute?"

I let out the breath I was holding and said, "Yeah, sure."

Gabe and I walked into the corner and I was just about to apologize when Gabe said, "Look, Jason, I invited Derrick because I really like him. We're all here to celebrate Iz's birthday and Sarah's and my upcoming nuptials. We *are not* here for you to become all macho and start stupid arguments. You hear me?"

I looked away because if I didn't, I would have punched Gabe in the face and then I would have to deal with Sarah. And if I thought Jade was scary when she was angry, I can only imagine what Sarah's like. I looked back at Gabe, and staring at him, I pointed in the direction of Ryder and Derrick and said, "Fine, but if I hear that asshole motherfucker talk about his girl one more time while we're here, I will fuck his shit up. I'm not kidding, Gabe."

And for the life of me Gabe laughed. "All right, killer, let's go back."

Like what the fuck is his problem. I was surprised I was the only one getting pissed at Derrick mentioning the girl he was seeing while Ash was our friend.

I decided to get ready in Sarah and Gabe's room because I didn't know if Ash was still mad at me. I just wanted to give Ash her space. When we went to dinner, I tried to sit as far away from her as possible, but of course the only other available seat at the table was the one right across from her.

I tried not to look in her direction because Christ, my dick was already swelling up just catching a glimpse at what she was wearing. She had on this tight red dress that dipped in the front and showed off her perky tits. I couldn't help licking my lips because I wondered just how sweet they would taste in my mouth. I mean, I am a guy after all and Ashlynn was WOW!

She must have caught me staring because the next thing I knew she was wrapping her arms in front of her and I looked up and saw the most adorable scowl on her face. I tried to get out of it by winking at her, but *holy shit* because Ashlynn blushed. I mean her cheeks turned a shade of red. I didn't think she could help it because her scowl started to turn into a smile, but then she shook her head and the scowl appeared back on her face.

The asshole Derrick was sitting next to her and he leaned over and whispered something in her ear. I wondered what it was because she looked back at me and then turned to Derrick and shook her head.

The rest of dinner I tried not to jump over the table. Not only did I want to rip Ashlynn's dress off her body but I wanted to wipe the smile off Derrick's face. It was just pissing me off how he would giggle with her and poke her side. Meanwhile, this afternoon he was bragging about his new girl.

People tried to get me to join in on their conversations, but I just wasn't in the mood. I knew that once we got to the club, I would be able to really drink and enjoy myself, so I would just have to deal with the mess I was in until then.

Once we paid for dinner, we headed off to the club, Chateau Nightclub & Gardens. This hot server escorted us to our tables. Ryder had a table reserved for us, so after singing "Happy Birthday" to Iz and toasting to Sarah and Gabe, we started the long night ahead of us.

I thought the server would leave once she got all of our drinks, but she walked up to me and sat down on my lap. "I'm Samantha, so just let me know if I can get you anything else tonight." *Oh, I so knew what this means.*

Looking in Ashlynn's direction, I planned to rub it in her face but that asshole Derrick pulled her out onto the dance floor. I almost lost my shit right there but then I felt Samantha's hand going into my pocket and when I looked down, I saw she was putting her phone number there. I looked at her and she was looking back at me. She winked and then turned to the rest of the group and said, "I'll be back with your drinks."

I couldn't help it but I turned around to watch her ass shake as she left our table but then I saw red. A beautiful girl wearing red. She was swaying her hips and her head was hanging back while she was laughing and having a good time.

I had decided to just drink my beer and watch her for a little while. Maybe a little liquid courage would help me out but then I saw some cocksucker walk up behind her and grab her by the hips.

While one of my hands strangled the neck of the beer bottle, the other was clenching into a fist. I wanted to beat his fucking ass, but she seemed fine with it, so I let it go. They started grinding into one another and danced for a couple of seconds and then something happened.

He had turned her around and was trying to kiss her but I saw her hands on his chest trying to push him away. I was immediately out of my seat walking towards them. It felt like I couldn't get there fast enough. I was pushing people out of the way to get to Ashlynn. He kept trying to kiss her but she managed to push him away and said, "I'm not interested." The second she turned her back, he grabbed her by the wrist and I fucking lost it. Within seconds I got him to let go of Ashlynn and I punched that guy right in his nose.

He immediately fell to the floor and I yelled, "Keep your hands off my girl, you motherfucker!" The club was so loud that nobody else noticed except for Ashlynn, myself, and that bastard. After he got up and left, I looked over in the direction of Ashlynn and saw her chest was rising and falling really fast and her eyes were bulged out, staring at me.

I walked over to her and instantly wrapped her in my arms. I couldn't help but smell her, and holy shit, she reminded me of the summer time, and then I started thinking about her in a bathing suit, her in a bra and panties, and then her in nothing. I knew she could probably feel my throbbing dick against her stomach but she didn't even flinch. I pulled away from her and looked in her eyes and said, "Are you okay?"

She just nodded her head and said, "Thanks." And what she did next completely stunned the shit out of me.

Ashlynn picked up my right hand, the one I used to punch that motherfucker, and without taking her eyes off me, she kissed my hand. The second her lips touched my hand I completely lost it. I grabbed Ash by the hips and pushed her up against the wall in the corner of the club and without thinking, I kissed her. I couldn't hold it in any longer. I needed to kiss her. I had waited so long to feel her lips up against mine. To feel her tongue dance with mine. To feel her body pressed up against mine.

And my god, was the wait worth it.

Her lips were plump and soft and tasted like vanilla. They tasted just how I imagined Ash would taste. Sweet and sexy all in one. Her body was made to fit up against mine. It started to get me thinking about how I would feel inside of her sweet little pussy.

If it was at all possible, my dick got harder and I started to grind up against her. At that point I thought she was going to push me away but Ash grabbed me by my shoulders and ground into me as well. I started to lick my way down her neck and felt the vibrations of her moans against my lips. She started to kiss along my jaw and then whispered, "Jason," in my ear and my heart instantly dropped. I pushed away from her because as much as I wanted to, I couldn't screw up with Ash like that.

The look in her eyes nearly destroyed me because for a second I thought she was going to cry, but then her face turned cold, and before I knew it she was slapping me hard against the face. "Fuck you, Jason!" she screamed.

I tried to grab her arm to apologize and explain to her why I couldn't do this, but Jade walked up to me and said, "I think you've messed up enough. Don't you think, Jason?" She didn't give me time to say anything because she was in the process of running after Ashlynn.

Chapter 2

Ashlynn

Jason was acting pretty weird all day. He seemed like he was nervous on the plane ride over, so I just listened to music and read my book. I thought maybe he was nervous about being on a plane because his knee kept bouncing up and down and he either had his lower lip in his mouth, nibbling on it, or he was biting his nails. The first was extremely sexual, so I was glad when he started biting his fingernails, because I dried up within a millisecond.

I decided to give him his space but then he went and got ready in Sarah and Gabe's room for Isabelle's birthday dinner. As soon as he walked out of the door with his suit, my stomach began to rumble and my heart beat quickened.

I thought about whether I had done anything wrong, but in all honesty I hadn't really talked to him that much lately. When we first started as freshmen, Jason was always coming over to hang out with Jade and I. We were either studying and doing homework together or we were going out to the frat parties and getting really drunk and lying around in bed the following day because we were suffering deathly hangovers.

But here we were three years later. I was finally deciding to get over my super huge crush on Jason Williams. Jade had always rooted for us because she said that we were perfect together. She said we evened one another out, and as much as I hoped that would happen, it hadn't yet, and I don't think it ever will.

When he left my room without looking back to go change in another room, I was hurt but decided to take a deep breath and move on.

Going to the restaurant, I decided to sit down and I saw Jason look at me with wide eyes. I patted the seat next to me and bobbed my head towards him but he shook his head. I'm not going to lie—it really hurt—but it was fine with me because the only other seat available was the one directly across from me. *Even better.*

Even though I was pissed because he'd been acting weird all day, he was still the only man that got my heart to skip a beat and beat twice as fast all at the same time. He gave me butterflies and goose bumps. He made me nervous and I wanted to crawl out of my skin even while he made me feel so comfortable in my own skin and being myself.

Derrick walked in right after Jason, so he sat next to me during dinner. I was relieved that I had Derrick by my side. He would be able to calm me down and get my mind off of Jason.

Feeling Derrick lean into me, he whispered in my ear, "Wipe that frown off your face, Ash."

I turned to Derrick and attempted to smile but I couldn't. I was hurt by the way Jason was acting and I didn't understand what I had done wrong. I went back to looking down at my plate and playing with my food.

I could feel eyes on me. I looked up to see Jason staring at me. I thought when I looked into his eyes they were going to be filled with anger and rage, but they weren't. His pupils were dilated and I could see that he was breathing a little bit harder than normal. His eyes were on mine and then I noticed that he took in the rest of my appearance and stopped on my breasts.

My red dress had a deep cut in the front so the girls were on display and ready for some action. The second I saw his eyes stop there my nipples instantly tightened and I got the chills. My arms were covered in goose bumps and I could feel my panties getting moistened. I could feel a throb starting so I attempted to cross my legs to relieve some of the pressure but nothing was working.

I started to get really self-conscious because I just wanted to jump over that table into his lap and kiss him, so I wrapped my arms around myself to get him to stop. I knew if he looked at me any longer with that look in his eyes, I wouldn't have cared where we were.

I saw him shake his head and then he looked back up into my eyes and I swear it was almost as if he could hear my thoughts, because he winked at me and gave this crooked grin. I couldn't help it anymore and my face automatically blushed.

I smiled up at him through my eyelashes but then I remembered that Jason would never want me that way. So I shook those thoughts from my mind and was back to a look of disappointment.

I didn't think anybody else noticed our little whatever it was, but Derrick leaned over and said, "You might want to drink some ice cold water, because the way you two are looking at each other, well, I'm surprised you guys aren't in the bathroom right this very minute."

I turned to him and I wanted to slap the smile off his face, but then a little part of me wondered if Jason did want me. I was beginning to psych myself out but I turned to look at Jason and he had a huge scowl on his face, so I knew that Derrick's assumptions were wrong.

I turned back to him and shook my head, but he leaned in again and whispered, "You didn't see his reaction earlier to what I said."

"What did you say?"

Derrick shrugged his shoulders and with a sneaky grin plastered on his face he said, "Well, the guys asked me how I'm doing and I told them that I was in a new relationship. I just wanted to see Jason's reaction to it and he went bananas. He started screaming at me and defending you. I honestly thought you guys would be attending my funeral but Ryder told him to calm down."

Derrick laughed. "Anyway, Gabe walked him away from us and talked to him. I had asked for Ryder and Gabe's help with the whole thing because I wanted to see for my own two eyes whether or not Jason had feelings for you. While Gabe talked to him, Ryder and I kept laughing. Then we almost lost it when we heard Jason yelling at the top of his lungs about why am I here on the trip and if I mentioned one more thing about my new relationship, he was going to beat my ass."

I just shrugged and let out a breath. My arms slumped down into my lap and I looked down. Derrick wrapped his arm around me. "Then why won't he make a move or something?"

Derrick kissed me on the cheek. "Ash, that boy really likes you. I mean, *really* likes you but I don't know why he won't show you. Maybe he's like an onion where you have to peel back the layers one at a time for him to open up to you or something."

I turned to Derrick and just started laughing. "Really? You're going to use a *Shrek* analogy right now?"

Derrick's eyes got huge and then he lightly nudged me. "Hey, come on now, Ash! Don't go judgin' and hatin' on my favorite movie of ALL time!"

Again I just laughed. Derrick always knew how to cheer me up.

Poking my dimples, he said, "That's what I like to see. Now come on, girlfriend, we're going to make Jason a really jealous man tonight! You with me?"

I peeked at Jason out of the corner of my eye and saw he was looking at me. I turned back to Derrick and wrapped my arms around him and kissed him on the cheek. "Most definitely!"

Derrick and I touched and flirted for the remainder of dinner. I swear I could see smoke coming from Jason's direction but I inwardly giggled and started becoming a little more courageous. Of course the alcohol was also helping with that little part.

After we got to the club and said congratulations and everything, we ordered our drinks. As soon as I saw the waitress, I wanted to rip her hair out. She was checking Jason out.

My stomach instantly tightened and I wanted to throw up but after Derrick and I ordered our drinks he pulled me out onto the dance floor. Derrick wrapped his arms around my waist and we started grinding into one another and just having a good time.

We danced for a few more songs and then Derrick whispered in my ear, "That boy is fuming, Ash." We both started to giggle and I expertly looked behind me and saw Jason was about to crack.

I looked back at Derrick and hugged him. "Thanks, Derrick."

He smiled at me. "Anytime, chickee. Well, now that my evil plan is done, I'm going to go find my man."

I kissed him on the cheek. "I'll see you later."

Derrick's back was to me as he was walking away but he cocked his head toward me and said, "I'll see you tomorrow morning," then blew an air kiss at me.

I stood there for all of two seconds when a cute guy asked me to dance with him. I just smiled and nodded because the plan was getting a lot better. I began to wrap my arms around his neck but he put his hands at my waist and spun me around so my back was to his front. I could feel his erection pressed up against me and I started to get a little nervous.

I figured I could dance with him for one song and then be done with it. *I mean, it's only three minutes, right?* Well, three minutes of pure torture.

He ground into me and it was really rough and uncomfortable. He started moving his hands to my lady area and I tried to get him to stop. I guess he took that as an invitation because he spun me around and pressed me to him and then he tried to kiss me. I tried to push him away but he held onto me tightly.

I managed to step down on his foot with my high heel and pushed him off me. He started fuming and I started to walk away from him saying, "I'm not interested." As soon as the words left my mouth, I turned around to walk away from him but he grabbed my wrist and yanked me back.

I was just about to start screaming but somebody got him to release me and then I heard a fist slamming into the asshole's face. I turned around just in time to see Jason standing over the guy and yelling, "Keep your hands off my girl, you motherfucker!"

I looked around to see if security was coming, but nobody was. The club was so loud that you couldn't hear it. I looked back at Jason and he looked like he was going to murder the guy.

I couldn't move.

I couldn't form words.

I couldn't believe that Jason actually felt something for me. I was just about to say something when Jason turned to me and wrapped me in his arms. A part of me was nervous about how he was going to act but the second he touched me, everything else evaporated.

I felt safe.

I wrapped my arms around his neck and took a few breaths in and out. I could feel his erection pushing into my belly and I started to get butterflies. It turned me on and I was curious. I was about to kiss his neck when he put me at arm's length and looked into my eyes.

"Are you okay?"

Keeping eye contact, I nodded my head and managed to whisper, "Thanks." My heart was beating so fast and I wasn't breathing normally.

Jason dropped his hands and started to step away but I grabbed the hand that he used to punch the guy with and lifted it to my lips. I could see he was breathing really fast from the way his chest was heaving up and down.

Without taking my eyes off his, I pressed my lips to his hand. I figured it was now or never and I decided to go with now. I didn't care about the consequences or any of that. It didn't matter.

I was just getting ready to move my lips away when I heard him mumble under his breath, "Fuck it," and then he pushed me up against the wall and his lips were on mine.

Everything else vanished. All I saw was Jason. All I heard was the heavy breathing and teeth clenching and the moaning and groaning. All I felt was Jason's erection pushing against me and his hands roaming all over me.

He started to go on an exploration of my body. Fingers pushing into my hips, lips sucking my neck, and his tongue flicking my earlobes and sucking them into his mouth.

I wanted to explore him as well, so I began to kiss along his jaw and trail kisses up to his ear. I whispered, "Jason," in his ear, and before I knew it he was pushing himself away from me. I thought he was going to drag me out of the club but I looked up into his eyes and he looked scared. Scared shitless.

I knew it was too good to be true, that Jason would ever have feelings for me. He looked into my eyes. "I can't, Ash."

The second he said my name I wanted to cry but I didn't care anymore. I took a deep breath and then looked into his eyes. I pulled my hand back and slapped him so hard across his face. "Fuck you, Jason," I screamed.

As soon as I slapped Jason I wanted to apologize but I was just so pissed off and hurt that he'd pushed me away like that. He treated me like garbage and I didn't deserve that. Every step I took away from him I wanted to turn around but he didn't want me—that was very obvious. I didn't think this mess could get any worse but apparently I was wrong.

Jade told me our freshman year that Jason's life growing up was pretty hard. Their dad was always putting Jason down and if Jason got a 3.9 in school or made varsity his sophomore year in baseball their dad would belittle him and say, "Well, why couldn't you get a 4.0?" or "Why couldn't you have made varsity your freshman year?"

Jade told me because she wanted me to get a sort of understanding why Jason acts the way he does. I understood it but I didn't condone it. I was also not allowed to ever say anything because Jade said that if Jason ever found out I knew he would probably never talk to her again.

While the background information answered so many of the questions I had about Jason it also brought up so many more and they weren't for Jason.

All of my questions were for Jade.

I wondered what living with someone like that would do to her. How would it affect her in life?

Love?

Relationships?

Friendships?

I ran out of the club and before I knew it, Jade was behind me yelling my name. "Ashlynn!"

I turned around just in time for her to hug me and murmur sweet things in my ear. The second I wrapped my arms around her I just cried. We stood like that for a while, me crying and her trying to soothe me by rubbing her hands up and down my back.

Jade wanted me to go back into the club but I had had too much "excitement" for one night and decided to go back to the hotel. She told me I could sleep in her room but I thought some of us deserved to have some fun while in Vegas. I didn't even change out of my outfit. I just huddled under the covers and cried myself to sleep.

I couldn't believe it!

The second I decided to move on with my life and push my crush on Jason into the deepest part of my soul he calls me, "his girl," punches some asshole in the face defending me, creams my panties with just his lips on mine, his tongue on my neck licking and sucking, and then breaks my heart all over again.

I just can't believe this huge mess that I have created. I wish that I could have told Jason how I felt our freshman year of college and said, "Screw it." But nooo! I have to have a secret crush on him and let it consume my life and then have a "fake" boyfriend.

I mean am I that desperate to try and attempt to get him to notice me?

I guess so.

I was woken up later to someone yelling and others trying to calm the person down. I thought it was just another drunken idiot but then I heard the person say, "Ash," and I automatically knew it was Jason.

I jumped out of bed and turned on the bedside light. I didn't want to but I opened the door to our room and saw Gabe and Ryder trying to take Jason to Sarah and Gabe's room, but the second he heard our door open he turned around and smiled at me.

I wanted to slap that smile right from his beautiful face. He must have been able to read my mind because his smile quickly disappeared and then he was wobbling over to me.

Before I could say anything he was cradling my face in his hands and wiping my face, whispering over and over, "I'm so sorry, Ash," in a drunken slur.

I thought I had finished crying but I closed my eyes and more tears escaped.

I felt limp and numb, because for the longest time this mess was mine to carry but now Jason knew. I mean, I don't think he knew exactly how deeply I felt about him, but now he knew something was going on.

Gabe and Ryder started to walk over to us but I put my hand up to let them know that everything was going to be okay. At least for tonight.

After they left the hall, Jason pulled away and put his hand in mine and we walked back into our room together. I thought he was going to let go of my hand but he walked me into the bathroom and picked me up and sat me down on the counter. He walked out of the room for a minute and then walked back in with my makeup removal wipes.

Taking one out, he cradled my face in his hand and my eyes instantly closed. He applied the wipe to my face and removed all of the mascara that I knew was all over my face. When he was satisfied with the job, he threw the wipe away and picked me up. Without releasing me back onto the floor, he walked us over to my bed and laid me down.

I thought he was going over to his bed, but he turned the bedside lamp off and crawled in after me. He nestled up next to me and wrapped an arm around my waist. After kissing my neck, Jason whispered, "I'll fix this mess, Ash. I promise."

Chapter 3

Jason

The second Ash ran off I didn't know what to do. I stood in the same position she left me in for a few seconds, wondering how I was going to tell her why I couldn't do this between us. I wanted to tell her how I would kick myself every single second, minute, hour of every day because I couldn't be with her.

I started to run off in the direction of Ashlynn and Jade but Ryder walked up to me and placed a hand on my chest. "Not right now, man." I immediately stopped dead in my tracks and my head slumped over in defeat.

Up until Ryder met Isabelle, he was a huge player. In fact, I think he was getting more pussy than I was and that's saying something. I swear he could have a different girl every day for four years of college and there would still be remaining girls for the rest of us pathetic fucks who hadn't gotten all pussy-whipped and fallen in love yet.

That's just how easy it was for him. However, the second he met Isabelle everything changed. That motherfucker was pussy-whipped from the get go and it was kind of hysterical. Anyone with eyes could see how he felt about her. I saw him watch her the entire time she first walked into the café with Sarah and I knew I just had to be a dick to him.

It was like perfect timing when Isabelle started choking. I immediately got up from my seat and started to pat her back because I just wanted to see what the dipshit would do. Of course I didn't think about how Ash would react to it and I was surprised when I saw her flinch when I touched Iz.

While Iz was gorgeous, Ash was, well, she was something.

Ryder looked like he was going to turn into the Incredible Hulk and fuck my shit up so I just gave him this sly grin. Once Ash saw my face I saw her calm down so it was all good in the motherfuckin' hood.

I also had to push his buttons when I spotted Ryder and Isabelle at the bar with Ash. I looked at her and she laughed and said, "Go get 'em, tiger." We all knew Ryder had a major crush on Iz, but that girl was fuckin' blind because he practically was at her beck and call. Of course the secrets came out about how her mom was a huge bitch and secretly Jade and I could relate.

However as soon as I saw Ryd carry her out of the bar like a fuckin' caveman I knew that was it and he was off the market. It just took a girl who wasn't on her knees waiting to suck dick for that prick to fall in love. I knew he would do anything for that girl and that's how I would feel about Ash for the rest of my life.

Unfortunately, I could never put my thought into play. I mean, technically, I could, but I wanted Ash to be happy and I knew she wouldn't get that with me. In fact I was certain of it because up until Jade and I left for our freshman year of college, my life had been a mess. *Oh, who the fuck am I trying to kid? It still is.*

Ryder grabbed me by the shoulder. Looking up into his eyes, he nodded in the direction of our table. Sitting down at the booth, I picked up my bottle and took a good healthy gulp. Placing the bottle back down on the table, I looked over at Ryder and waited for the interrogation to begin.

He took a sip of his beer then set it down on the table in front of us. He looked over at me and quirked an eyebrow. "You want to talk about what just happened between you and Ash?"

I just shrugged. "I don't really know what to say."

In a more serious tone he said, "Well, let's start with what exactly happened, Jason."

I was starting to get really pissed off with Ryder. It wasn't really any of his business.

A little bit louder I said, "Like I said, Ryder, I don't really know what happened." I wanted to try and explain it to him but he got his girl. I didn't.

Getting up from his seat, Ryder walked over to me and placed an arm around me. "Well, since you don't know what just happened out there then I'll tell you what happened. Some jackass who hasn't seen what's been right in front of him got jealous and made out with a girl who has had a crush on him since forever."

Looking over at him, I began to say something but he put his finger up to stop me and continued on. "You gave that girl hope and you crushed her all over again. I don't know what the fuck your problem is, because I notice the way you look at her, and I can tell you right now it's the same way I look at Isabelle. I just don't know what the fuck your problem is, man."

Looking over at Ryder, I shook my head. *I thought I was hiding my feelings pretty well. Apparently not.*

Letting out a deep breath, I said, "I've liked Ash for a long time but I've tried to stay away and just be her friend because I'm such a mess and she doesn't deserve that. So I've been quiet but when she kissed my hand ... Ryder, I fucking lost it. I just went crazy and she didn't stop me."

Putting my hands on the top of my head, I started pulling my hair. Yelling, "FUCK," at the top of my lungs, I looked over at Ryder.

He scrunched his eyebrows together. He took a deep breath. "You like her?"

I just laughed and shook my head. "Fuck, no. The word *like* doesn't even come close to how I feel about that girl."

He leaned in closer. "You love her?"

I stared at him. I began to think about it and then looked over at Ryder. "I'm not sure how to answer that question honestly, Ryd."

Half of Ryder's mouth came up in a grin. "I think you just did."

I smiled at him but just then I felt something in my gut and I knew I was in trouble. I looked over at Ryder and his Adam's apple bobbed up and down and then my heart plummeted. I took a deep breath and turned around just in time to see Jade and Isabelle marching up in our direction and they were fuming. I swear I could see smoke coming from their ears and their eyes were glaring daggers right at me.

Isabelle walked over and sat down on Ryder's lap, wrapping her arms around his neck. She smiled and kissed him and then she turned to me and the look she gave was scary as hell. I think I would have rather cut my own dick off than have her look at me that way ever again.

Jade sat down next to me. She just looked at me and shook her head. That's all she had to do because I knew she was disappointed with me and no words could describe how pissed she was at me. She knew I had a huge thing for Ashlynn, but while I had huge balls, they just weren't big enough to tell Ash how I felt about her.

Putting my head down, I sighed. Long and hard. *Jesus Christ, now my dick is starting to swell.*

This was all such a huge mess and I didn't know how to fix it. I didn't even know where to begin in trying to make an attempt. I feel like I just keep digging a bigger hole for myself and I don't know how to get out of it.

In the back of my mind I could hear Jade and Iz talking about the situation between Ashlynn and myself but I didn't care. I just kept thinking about Ash.

Once Isabelle and Jade gave their opinions, they went back onto the dance floor. However Isabelle stopped and looked at Ryder, waiting for him. I looked over at Ryder and he put a finger up in her direction and said, "I'll be out there in a second sweetheart." The second he said, "sweetheart," Isabelle was like a puddle at his feet. Her eyes twinkled and the smile that went across her face was indescribable, and it was one I wanted desperately to cause on Ash's face.

When Jade and Isabelle were out of hearing distance, Ryder leaned in and said, "Look, I know what you're going through. It's the exact same thing Isabelle and I went through but look at where we are." He must have sensed that I was going to say something because he placed a finger up and motioned for me to keep quiet so he could continue. "I know something happened to you, Jason, I'm just not sure what. But I can tell you that Ashlynn is a lot stronger than you think she is and I know that she would go to the ends of the earth for you."

I looked up at him. "How can you be so sure on your observation of Ash, Ryder?"

Without taking his eyes off me he smiled and said, "Because I would do that for Isabelle without any hesitation."

At that moment, Isabelle walked up and grabbed Ryder's hand and started pulling him along. "Come on, munchkin."

Ryder looked over at me and raised an eyebrow. I just mock saluted him, and chuckling, I said, "Understood, *munchkin*."

Ryd just gave me the finger and pinched Isabelle's ass as they walked back to the dance floor.

Even though I felt like complete shit for what happened with me and Ashlynn, I was extremely happy for Ryder and Isabelle. I started to think about what Ryder had to say about comparing himself and Isabelle to Ashlynn and myself. I know without a doubt that Ashlynn is strong enough to do whatever she puts her mind to but I'm just not sure if I'm strong enough.

As soon as the lovebirds were out of sight I drank the rest of my beer. I was just about to get another one but Samantha, the waitress, walked up and placed another one down for me and winked before she left. That's how the rest of the night went. Samantha bringing me drinks and me trying to drink myself into oblivion.

After a couple more drinks everything started to blur together. At one point I was down on the dance floor, grinding into Samantha. She was really hot but she was nothing compared to Ash because Ashlynn was beautiful. She kept whispering in my ear for us to go in the back for some privacy but I knew what that meant. I kept shaking my head but my resolve was quickly fading.

I instantly sobered up when Samantha wrapped her arms around me and leaned in for a kiss. I moved my head down and the second her lips met mine I felt nothing. All that I felt and remembered was Ash and how hurt I knew she was. Samantha started to deepen the kiss by swiping her tongue along my lower lip, but I moved away from her. Placing her hands on her hips, she looked up at me with disgust.

Shaking my head I said, "I'm sorry, I just … I can't do this, Samantha."

Snarling, she said, "It's because of that bitch from earlier, isn't it?"

I started to get really pissed off and met her eyes. "Call her a bitch one more time and see what happens."

She just giggled. "Your loss, asshole." She walked away from me. Of course she had to shake her ass, look back at me and wink. But at least the bitch left.

Before I could think about where I wanted to go my feet were moving. One in front of the other. Walking back up to our table to grab my wallet, I saw Ryder and Isabelle and Gabe and Sarah. Of course they were snuggled up in one another's arms.

They must have heard me because Ryder looked over in my direction and asked, "You ready?"

"Yeah, I'm getting ready to leave."

I didn't even get to finish my sentence before Isabelle was jumping up saying, "Oh no, Jason, don't even think about it. You'll be staying in our room tonight."

I looked over at Ryder, but he nodded his head in agreement with Isabelle. *I feel like such a dick for cockblocking Ryder and Isabelle but what are my other options?* I figured since I wouldn't be able to apologize to Ashlynn tonight then I might as well have a few more drinks and get completely wasted. Nobody agreed with my decision, but I didn't give a shit.

After hailing a cab, we finally made it back to the hotel. Ryder and Gabe had to help me because I started wobbling around and slurring my words together. I started to pull out my swipe card but Isabelle placed a hand on top of mine. Looking into my eyes she said, "Remember, Jason, you're staying with us tonight."

I started shaking my head saying, "No," but Gabe said, "Come on, man. You just need to lie down and go to sleep. You'll have a shitty hangover tomorrow but at least you'll have a clearer head than you do right now."

He started to pull me down the hall but I said, "I want to see Ash. Ash. ASH!"

I tried to push Gabe and Ryder off me because I needed to see Ashlynn but they began to pull me down the hall. We didn't get more than five feet before I heard a door open. My heart jumped up and down and I turned around in the hopes that maybe, just maybe, the door opening would be Ash's. I pushed off Ryder ad Gabe to see Ash and the view broke my heart. Ash's mascara was all over her face, her eyes were twice their normal size, and her nose was all red from crying.

I staggered over to Ash and wrapped her head in my hands, whispering, "I'm so sorry, Ash," over and over again. It broke my heart that she was crying over me. Because of me. That's the reason I can't date Ash, because I'll break her heart over and over again. It's really that simple. It's not that I want to, but with a past like mine I question everything and I can't hurt someone the way my dad hurt my mom, Jade, and myself.

Seeing more tears escape her eyes, I thought I was going to cry for a second but I gulped and swallowed them away. I could hear footsteps from behind me. At first they were walking towards us but then they quickly vanished. I just kept running my thumbs up and down Ash's cheeks on either side, trying to comfort her. I wanted to kiss her again, but I didn't think that would go over too well with her. So I moved away and put her hand in mine and walked us back into our room together.

I couldn't take the mascara all over her face any longer so as soon as we got into our room I walked her into the bathroom and placed her on the counter. I heard her breathing loudly but I needed to do this. I needed to show her that I could take care of her. In some sort of way, at least.

While I looked for her makeup removal wipes, I had an inner battle with myself. I wanted to show her that I could be who she wanted, but I also knew that I would end up hurting her the way my dad hurt my mom. I let the first win because I wanted her to be happy and I knew at least a small part of me could do that for her.

Walking back in the bathroom, I placed the cool wipe to her cheek and began to wipe off her black mascara. I wiped her cheeks, her nose, and both eyes. When I was satisfied with my clean-up job, I picked her up in my arms and walked her over to her bed so she could go to sleep. I walked over and turned off the bedside table lamp and then began to walk over to my bed but I stopped and turned.

I saw Ash's back and again I had a battle with myself but I decided to just go with it. I needed to be close to her even if only for a second before she pushed me out of her bed. So I sat down on her bed and scooted over to her and cradled her against me.

Kissing her on the neck, I whispered in her ear, "I'll fix this mess, Ash. I promise." I didn't get to hear what she had to say because before I knew it my eyes were closed and I was drifting off into a peaceful sleep.

***

I woke up with the world's worst hangover the following morning but I had the most beautiful girl wrapped up in my arms. Somehow during the night she'd turned so her body was facing me, so I took a few seconds to just look at her.

I always thought Ash was beautiful but there weren't words to describe how incredible she looked in the morning. *God, she is breathtaking.* Her hair was lying on the pillow and her mouth was opened just slightly and she made the most gorgeous little sounds. It wasn't snoring; more like purring.

As I stared at her I realized I wanted Ashlynn. I needed Ashlynn, and I knew exactly what I needed to do in order to get her. I was taking a leap of faith because I didn't know if she would agree to it, but if Ryder was right about Ashlynn, then I had nothing to worry about.

I figured today was a new day. A new start. A new beginning and I wanted to begin something, I'm not sure what exactly, but something with Ashlynn Miller.

Kissing her on the cheek, I quietly got up out of bed. I didn't want to wake her because I had a surprise for her. After relieving myself in the bathroom, I grabbed some aspirin and a bottle of water. Swallowing the pills and gulping down the bottle of water, I grabbed my cell phone and left the room.

Getting the phone number from reception I dialed.

"Airlines. How may I help you?"

Taking a few deep breaths I said, "I need to make a flight change."

After the conversation, I hung up the phone. Looking down, I could feel my heart beating so fast I thought I was going to pass out. Clicking my phone shut, I said, "I hope you know what exactly you're doing, Jason."

Taking one step at a time, I made my way back to mine and Ashlynn's room. I could hear moving around on the other side and knew Ashlynn was up. I wasn't sure if I was incredibly excited or scared shitless to walk into that room because I didn't know what would be waiting for me on the other side.

With shaky fingers, I got out my swipe card. *Come on, Jason, you can do this. Just walk through. It's only Ashlynn.* But she wasn't just any girl. She was *the* girl. My girl, or at least I hoped.

After getting the green light, I opened the door. Ash's back was to me and I saw that she was packing up her clothes. The second she heard the door open, I noticed she scrunched up a little bit from behind and jumped; almost like she was scared of me or what I was going to say. I could tell she was nervous. In this tiny voice she squeaked, "Jason …"

She was getting ready to say something but I cut her off. "You should probably pack up the rest of your stuff. Our flight leaves in a little while."

She was biting her lip but she let it go and her face automatically turned down in a frown. It looked almost like I punched her in the gut from the way she was reacting, but hopefully she wouldn't be acting like that for much longer.

I just hope I'm doing the right thing and not making a bigger mess for the both of us.

Chapter 4

Ashlynn

I thought I was going to wake up in Jason's arms, but I didn't. Although I did wake up with a horrible headache because of all the crying I had done the night before. Stretching and getting up from bed, I walked over to my makeup bag and searched for some type of Tylenol or Advil to relieve my headache.

Stumbling upon my makeup removal wipes, my tummy automatically started doing somersaults and flips because of the memories of Jason last night. At first I thought it was all a dream and I never wanted to wake up from it. It made me think that the horrible mess prior was so worth it because we came out to a beautiful thing afterwards.

Watching him as he wiped away the smeared mascara on my face, I could tell there was something in him that was changing, although I could tell there was a part of him that wanted to fight it every step of the way. Somehow, someway I was going to get through that barrier. I noticed it in his eyes when he was wiping away the mascara. He was biting his lower lip and scrunching his eyebrows together and kept shaking his head back.

I started to wonder if everything Jade had told me was only a small portion of what growing up in the Williams' household was like. I started to think back on the years at school and realized that not once did Mr. or Mrs. Williams ever visit their children.

Meanwhile my dad was always making surprise appearances. Sometimes I was kind of annoyed with it because on some occasions I was rather hung over but I was grateful my dad was always there for me. Jade and I were so close that my dad always included Jade and Jason in on whatever we were doing. Sometimes we would just go get something to eat or even go see a movie.

I thought it was really sweet when the school sent home gift basket order forms around midterm and finals time. Miraculously, Jade and Jason always received one but it was never from their parents. I knew they were from my dad but he never told me about it.

I also started to question if I was strong enough to help Jason with his struggles. I just didn't want to create a bigger mess for Jason to have to deal with and clean up. I wanted to help him, not hurt him.

Taking some Tylenol and a few sips of water, I started to get ready. Our flight back home would be leaving shortly. I wondered where Jason was, but maybe he just needed this time alone to think about things between us and where exactly we went from here like I was.

After taking my shower I just put on some jean shorts and a sweatshirt. I didn't bother washing my hair because I didn't feel like it. Today was my lazy day and I was welcoming it with open arms. I already felt like shit on the inside so why not look like shit?

I began to pack my bag when I heard the door unlock and begin to open. I thought I had calmed down but my chest started to heave up and down. I felt like I was going to have a panic attack or something. Yesterday Jason could have walked in here and I would have just felt my heart skip a beat and my face redden but today was the total opposite. I didn't know how to act around him. I couldn't just be myself because within the past 24 hours everything had changed between us.

I took a deep breath and slowly turned around and Jason was smiling at me. I opened my mouth and said, "Jason …" but he didn't let me finish.

It felt like someone ran me over, beat the shit out of me, and left me on the side of the road. I wanted to ask him what exactly happened last night. Where do we go from here? What do you want?

But I guess him cutting me off and saying, "You should probably pack up your stuff. Our flight leaves in a little while," was all he needed to say.

He wanted to forget the last 24 hours, but I wouldn't. I would keep those memories for as long as I lived and cherish them under lock and key. I would remember that for the 24 hours we were in

Vegas that things between Jason and I were different. A complete 180.

Things were quiet between us while we both packed up our stuff to head back home. When I finished packing, I sat on the uncomfortable hotel bed and remembered last night when Jason snuggled up next to me and kept me close to him. He kept me safe and comforted me. And in that he gave me hope.

Pulling out my Kindle, I began to read a book I had downloaded on the flight over. I was still reading when Jason walked over to me and nudged me with his foot. I looked up at him, confused, and he said, "Ready, Ash?"

Oh yeah, back to reality where shitty things do happen to good people, unlike books that are written for make-believe and where your dreams really do come true. Where your prayers are actually answered and you truly can have it all.

I just nodded my head and quietly said, "Yeah, I guess."

I got up from the bed and started to grab my bag when Jason said, "I got it, Ash."

I looked down because I couldn't bear to see the look in his eyes when I whispered, "No, you don't. You never did." With that I picked up my bag and we both left the room, checked out of the hotel, and hailed a cab.

Every step that I took felt like I was being stabbed in the heart and someone was twisting it. I just wished that I had a magical clock where I could rewind time and figure out where it all went wrong and change it so maybe right now could be different.

Instead of waking up alone, I could be waking up in Jason's arms and kissing him. Where we could stay in bed all day and change our flight time because we got carried away. Where we could get to know one another on a different level besides that of friends. Where we could go back to school as a couple and see where *this* took us.

Whatever path it led us down, because good or bad, right or wrong it would be amazing. No matter what way it ended: with him forever or with him for only a short while I would be changed in some sort of way for the rest of my life. All because of Jason Williams.

Walking into the airport lounge, my heart was beating out of its chest because I didn't want to board the plane. I didn't want to go back to Maryland and in five years, ten years from now look back and think that our short trip in Vegas was only a dream and how I wished I would have never woken up. Because like books and movies, dreams are more often than not better than reality.

We started walking in the direction of our gate and as I started to turn, Jason put a hand on my upper arm, signaling for me to stop. Stopping, I slowly looked up into his eyes and he was looking at me with the hint of a smile on his face. Out of the corner of my eye, I saw something white was waving below us and I looked down. I noticed that he was holding two airplane tickets and I wondered when he snooped into my bag and got mine.

I quickly pulled my purse off of my shoulder and unzipped it. I started digging around and noticed that my ticket was still inside my wallet, folded up and hidden away; like my short time with Jason. I slowly looked up into Jason's eyes and tilted my head.

He shrugged his shoulders and let out a laugh. "I just thought we could use another vacation."

I took hold of the plane tickets and read that we were headed to Florida. A smile began to creep up on my face but then it quickly disappeared because I came to the realization that this vacation was just going to be Jason and me.

Alone.

Together.

I started to bite my lower lip because I was nervous. Jason must have noticed it and sensed how I was feeling. Holding up the plane tickets, Jason said, "I thought we could hang out, Ash. Just the two of us. No one else."

I was still silent, so Jason said, "It's my parents' vacation house. It's right by the edge of the ocean. If everything goes well, I thought we could stay for the rest of Spring Break." Pausing, he said, "That is, if you want to."

I began to open my mouth but no words were coming out. I was surprised I was still standing up, to be honest. And that I was breathing in and out.

Continuing, Jason said, "The reason I wanted to go to Florida is so I could explain some things to you. Explain about what exactly happened last night and get everything out on the table. No more surprises. No more secrets."

I started to think about what Jason just said. It was everything I wanted but I was scared of these secrets he was talking about.

To me it was okay.

To me it was perfect.

Perfectly okay.

Sucking in a shaky breath, I nodded my head and whispered, "Okay."

As soon as that one word left my lips, a smile came across Jason's face and his eyes brightened up. Nodding his head, he let out a breath and said, "Okay then," and grabbing my hand, we walked to our new destination.

***

On the flight over to Florida, Jason and I were pretty quiet. I texted Jade, letting her know that Jason and I had some things we had to straighten out and that I wouldn't be coming home today. She texted me back telling me to take my time and see what could happen between Jason and I.

Jade had these high hopes and not a care in the world. Me, on the other hand? I second guessed everything and questioned what exactly would happen. I wanted Jason but I was scared. Scared in the sense that I wasn't sure if I was strong enough to help Jason with the demons of his past. Scared to find out what exactly had happened to him and Jade as children.

Landing in Florida, we caught a cab and made our way over to Jason's parents' beach house. It was funny because Jason was laughing and smiling again. The way he was our night in Vegas when he attacked me with kisses up against the wall. It seemed like all we had to do was go on vacations for everything to be "normal" between us. But life isn't a vacation and at some point we have to get back to reality.

So as much as I was going to enjoy this vacation and my time alone with Jason, I was also nervous about getting back on that plane and going back to school. I didn't know which Jason would be getting on the plane with me. The Jason I had known since freshman year of college or the Jason that kissed me and made me feel like I was his and his only.

After Jason paid for the cab fare, he got our luggage and we walked up to the house. He got a key from underneath the front door mat and quickly unlocked the door. Opening the door, he said, "After you, milady."

Even though I was wearing jean shorts, I pretended I had on a Victorian dress and curtsied, saying, "Thank you, kind sir."

I walked in and heard Jason laughing behind me. I turned back to him and he was placing the luggage down on either side of him and then he lifted his arms and shrugged. "Do you want to look around?"

As soon as he closed the door, I began to get nervous. I could feel beads of sweat forming at the top of my forehead. I thought maybe Jason could hear my heart pounding out of my chest and see my fingers starting to twitch.

I shook the nervousness away and said, "Yeah, let's take a look around."

Jason showed me around the house, which was pretty simple. I mean, it was just a beach house that was all one level with a living room and kitchen along with three bedrooms. The living room was in the back of the house and there were large windows which showed a clear view of the crisp, clear ocean and the sand I couldn't wait to feel between my toes.

After showing me around the house, we made our way back into the kitchen. Jason was pulling out ingredients to make sandwiches. I walked over to him and nudged him on the shoulder. "Can I help?"

He laughed and said, "Yeah, I thought we could get a cooler ready and hang out at the beach for the rest of the day. Does that sound okay?"

I was busy making a sandwich and smiled. "That sounds amazing but Jason, I just wanted to know where I should stay."

He looked over at me said, "You're staying here, silly."

I shook my head and said, "I meant which bedroom I should stay in."

He was in the middle of spreading mustard on his sandwich when he dropped it and stuttered saying, "Oh, um, how about Jade's room?"

"Okay, that sounds good."

Jason nudged my shoulder and said, "How about you go get ready for the beach and I'll finish up here. Sound good?"

I just nodded my head and began to walk over to the front door to pick up my bag when I heard Jason say, "I'm really glad you're here, Ash."

I stopped in my tracks and smiled. Just turning my head back towards his direction, I said, "So am I, Jason."

Making my way back to Jade's room, I started to get nervous. Closing the door behind me, I sagged down to the floor and started hyperventilating. "Come on, Ash! This is what you wanted. Just play it cool and everything will be okay."

Psyching myself up, I dropped my bag on the bed and started going through it to get my bikini and then I realized I needed to shave. Thankfully, Jade had a bathroom in her room so I quickly shaved my legs and another area (wink, wink) and changed into my pink bikini and put on a pair of jean shorts.

I borrowed one of Jade's beach bags and put in a towel, sun screen, my Kindle, and a t-shirt. I thought about wearing the t-shirt but I opted against it. Grabbing some sunglasses, I walked out into the kitchen. Jason's back was to me and he was talking to himself. I couldn't really hear much of what he had to say. After packing up the cooler, he turned around and his jaw dropped to the floor.

Okay, not really, but it was pretty damn close.

I inwardly smiled and gave myself a pat on the back but on the outside I blushed like crazy. He was staring at me like he wanted to rip my clothes off but after a second he shook his head and said, "I better go get changed and then we can go to the beach."

In this tiny voice I squeaked, "Okay," and then proceeded to wait for him.

Jason didn't take any time at all and I almost lost my shit when he walked back into the kitchen with swim trunks on and nothing else. Well, except for the flip-flops on his feet and towel draped over his shoulder. I started from his feet and slowly worked my way up his incredible physique. *Who knew that a guy's feet could be so sexy? Neither did I.*

His stomach was, well, I have no words for it. He didn't *just* have a six pack, it was *wow my panties are soaked.* By the time I made it up to his face he was biting his lower lip and then I looked into his eyes and he winked at me. "Come on, Ash, let's go." I quickly grabbed my bag and Jason grabbed the cooler and we started to make our way down to the beach.

Thankfully there weren't that many people out so we had our alone time. I was both thankful and nervous because I didn't know how to act. We were going into a completely different territory and I didn't want to mess it up.

We walked a little bit and then settled down. Jason laid his towel out and then plopped down and started going through the cooler. I placed my bag down and took a deep breath. Getting my towel out, I laid it next to Jason's and then quickly unbuttoned and pulled down my jean shorts. I had bent over and when I stood up I noticed that Jason had a sandwich halfway to his mouth but he was staring at me. His pupils were dilated and he was breathing really heavily. In turn, I bit my lower lip and then Jason focused on that lower lip.

I giggled and said, "Is that sandwich good?"

Jason blinked a few times and then said, "I don't know. You want a bite?"

God, yes, I want a bite! I want to suck, lick, and nip! Fuck, I need to go into the cold, salty ocean water and cool down a bit! Okay, salty is not helping one bit, Ashlynn Paisley Miller!

I'm not exactly sure who I surprised more, myself or Jason when I nodded my head and leaned in to take a bite of his sandwich. I never took my eyes off his the entire time. I heard him take a deep breath and, just because I could, I moaned and said, "Best sandwich I've ever had."

I had just swallowed the bite when Jason dropped the sandwich and grabbed my face and kissed me. It took me a second but I moaned when he licked my lower lip and asked for entrance. I wrapped my arms around him and moved my head a little so we could deepen the kiss. The second our tongues touched I heard him moan, but just as quickly as he kissed me, he leaned back and said, "I'm going to go swim." And just like that he was up and walking towards the ocean.

I was stunned and couldn't believe that the same thing happened again, but this time I was beyond pissed. I was enraged.

His feet were just touching the ocean water when I ran up to him and spun him around. He looked at me and I could see that he thought I was going to slap him again but I pushed him. "Don't you dare, Jason Williams! You can't play these Jedi mind trick games with me. One second you're pushing me away and the next you're attacking me with kisses." I just started to tear up and lowered my head. Whispering, I said, "Please tell me you feel something too because this just isn't fair."

Jason placed a finger underneath my chin and lifted it so we were looking at one another. He looked like he was going to cry or scream or something. The reason I knew was because I felt the same exact way. I knew that my face mirrored his with the sad puppy dog eyes, the tears welling up and the biting of the bottom lip while the chin quivered.

Jason dropped his head in his hands and looked down at the golden sand below him. Lifting his head, he leaned in and lightly kissed me on the lips. Pulling away, he said, "I want this, Ashlynn, but I just can't. You're too important to me and I don't want to mess this up. I'm sorry."

Pushing him, I yelled, "What can't you do, Jason?" Looking out around us, I said, "Why the hell did you bring me here, then? You can't just play with people's emotions like this. It's not right!"

Trying to catch my breath, I shook my head. I turned back to my beach towel and plopped down. I thought staying in Florida would be different for us, but it wasn't. I thought he would whisk me away to this beautiful place and we would have a beautiful time. Instead, it had turned into a tornado disaster of a mess. I kind of wish we had just went back home because I couldn't deal with whatever this was between Jason and I for much longer.

I was drowning in my sorrows and feeling sorry for myself when I saw some feet stop in front of me as I played with the sand. I heard Jason say, "Get up, Ashlynn."

Looking up at him with his hands on his hips, looking so damn beautiful, I wanted to burst into tears, because I knew this was going to end before it even had the chance to begin.

Chapter 5

Jason

Just fuck me right now! Seeing Ash in that gorgeous pink bikini was wow! As soon as I saw her and the way her tits were just begging for attention, my dick was up front and center. I'm surprised she didn't say anything about my hard-on. At first I didn't think I could walk down to the beach because I felt like I needed to go back in the bathroom for a second or two, literally. I was as hard as cement. *Fuck!* That pales in comparison to how fucking hard I was.

I knew I couldn't let her out of my sight so I started to think about anything gross. Kids who pick their nose and eat the boogers. Dogs that lick their own assholes. Old men scratching their hairy, wrinkly balls. *Good boy, Hardy, you're down!*

I knew this whole thing was going to be a complete mess no matter what but I could give my balls for how little I cared. I was a selfish prick and

I was tired of hiding away my feelings for Ash. It's like I'm Dr. Jekyll and Mr. Hyde. On one side I'm trying to save her from a huge mess she doesn't need to be in. But the other side, the more dominant side at the moment, doesn't give a rat's ass because I'm too selfish and I just want Ash. The sickest part about it is that I'm so selfish I wonder sometimes if she could actually help me deal with everything going on in my life.

I feel like I'm suffocating and Ash is my oxygen. Not to be a complete girl in these next few seconds but she's the light in my darkness. The cookie to my cream. The baseball to my bat. She's ... my everything.

Just so we're clear, I don't care if you just judged me right then and there. Because a real man can wear pink. He can watch The Notebook *and find Ryan Gosling attractive as all hell. He can scream at the television and cry when* The Biggest Loser *winner is announced between sobs saying, "Yeah, you did!" I'm not saying I do that, but okay, you caught me. And heads up! If you tell anybody I won't be your book boyfriend. Just so we're clear on all counts.*

As soon as we found where we would be sitting at the beach I plopped down and started rummaging through the cooler. I needed to stick a sandwich in my mouth before I yanked off Ash's bikini top and sucked on her sweet, round nipple. I was just about to stick the sandwich in my mouth when motherfucking shit! Ash was shimmying out of her jean shorts and her tits were bouncing up and down. *Of course Hardy had to come back!*

My jaw dropped and I'm really positive that some drool was on the side of my mouth. She must have noticed the drool or something because she giggled and said, "Is that sandwich good?"

I knew she wouldn't, so I said, "I don't know. You want a bite?"

Ash had just sat down when I finished asking her the question and I could feel my heart beating out of its chest. I thought for sure she'd slap me on the arm and say something along the lines of, "Oh my God, Jason," or, "Ha-ha, very funny." But she nodded her head and grabbed ahold of my wrist. Without taking her eyes off me, she took a bite of my sandwich. *Shit pearls, she moaned.*

I couldn't form simple words because all of my blood had rushed to my cock but I was gentlemanly enough to let her swallow her bite and then I just lost my shit completely. I grabbed her face and kissed the living fuck out of her. I was about to just take her right then and there but then everything came crashing down on me and said, "I'm going to go swim."

I wanted to cut my own dick off for doing that to her again. It's like as soon as I feel happy I know she'll be miserable. I was just about to touch the water when Ash spun me around. I knew she was pissed because you could practically see the smoke coming from her ears and the way she was puffing out her breaths. I started to prepare myself for the smack across the face that I knew was coming but she pushed me instead. Poking a finger in the middle of my chest, she said, "Don't you dare, Jason Williams! You can't play these Jedi mind trick games with me. One second you're pushing me away and the next you're attacking me with kisses."

I wanted to grab her in my arms and take away all of the pain I knew I was causing her but then I heard her whisper, "Please tell me you feel something too, because this just isn't fair."

Taking a deep breath, I put a finger underneath her chin and lightly kissed her on the lips. "I want this, Ashlynn, but I just can't. You are too important to me and I don't want to mess this up. I'm sorry." The words stung like a complete bitch but they had to be said. I had finally made my choice. I had finally ripped off the bandage.

I needed her to know that we could never be anything besides friends. That's why I had brought her here. I'm not sure if I needed it more for me or for her. But why then did I feel like there was a pit in my stomach that something just wasn't right? When you rip off the bandage it hurts, but you feel like you accomplished something. However, with this matter I think I just made a bigger mess than before and I knew in that moment what I wanted.

Ash had just sunk down on her beach towel looking so forlorn and I knew that the decision I was going to make would change everything. She was pushing the sand around in between her fingers and toes when I stopped in front of her and said, "Get up, Ashlynn." She looked up at me and I knew she was going to cry, but she stood up on wobbly legs. She was getting ready to open her mouth when I hoisted her up on my shoulders and walked her back to the beach house. *Cave man style.*

She was smacking my back and saying, "Put me down, Jason. Put me down," but little did she know that I was never going to let go of her. I was never going to put her down, but she had to know. I had to tell her.

Making my way into the beach house with Ash on my shoulders, I dropped her on the sofa in the living room and started pacing back and forth. I knew I needed to tell her. She deserved this but I just didn't know how to go about it.

She was getting ready to say something when I placed a finger to her lips and said, "I need to tell you something, Ashlynn." With my finger still on her luscious lips, she nodded. Without thinking, I kissed her because I wasn't sure if it would be the last or one of many, but the way she was looking at me gave me the courage to finally speak up.

"Jade's and my childhood was pretty fucked up. Dad was always belittling me and pushing me to work extremely hard. Even when I did succeed in something, he would put me down and degrade me. I kind of learned to look past the verbal abuse because he didn't matter to me all that much. But the physical abuse was a completely different story."

I heard Ash gasp and she was about to say something when I shushed her and said, "He's a drunk, but he's one of the top attorneys in the country so he got away with a lot of bullshit. When we were little, there were little shoves here or there, but as we got older, the physical abuse got a hell of a lot worse. Jade missed curfew once. I think we were in middle school and he was about to kick her

67

in the side when I pushed her out of the way to protect her. Needless to say, I wasn't able to go to baseball practice for a week, but he never hit Jade again.

"The sick bastard knew how to hit me without showing physical evidence where it would be visible. It was all along my chest or legs or ribs. I stopped counting how many times I was in the hospital for chipped teeth, cracked ribs, and broken bones."

I took a breather because this was really hard for me to say. I had never told anyone this before and neither had Jade. We were both ashamed and we knew no one would ever believe us. Top Defense Attorney vs. two teenagers. Hands down, no competition. I also knew that it was a lot for Ashlynn to take in.

I wanted to look up at her but I didn't know what emotion would cross her face, then I heard her whisper, "Where was your mom?"

I looked up at her face and saw tears streaming down. As much as I wanted to wipe them away, I had to keep going on with my explanation. "I don't know. Probably passed out somewhere because of too many cocktails. The spa or lunches with the ladies. Working on the board. Doesn't really matter because she wouldn't have done anything, either way.

"Not only was my dad physically and verbally abusive with his children but he cheated on his wife and had numerous affairs. I wouldn't be surprised if Jade and I had brothers and sisters out there somewhere."

Pausing, I sucked in a breath before I looked up into Ash's eyes. "That's why we can't be together, Ashlynn. My life has been a mess and I don't want to end up like my dad. Beating up his children. Cheating on his wife. You don't deserve that. So there you have it. My sob story. My reason for pushing you away."

She walked over to me and sat down beside me. "I don't understand why you're pushing me away, Jason. You're kind and funny. You're smart. You're beautiful."

Cupping her face between my hands, I said, "Because I don't do relationships. I have sex with girls, I don't fall in love with them. I keep that barrier up because I can't turn out like my dad. I also know that I would never have children because I would never want to ruin their childhoods and their lives the way both of my parents destroyed mine and Jade's. I won't allow it. Kids deserve to run around in the yard and get ice cream from the ice cream truck. They deserve to act silly and get messy and sticky. What they don't deserve is dealing with physical and verbal abuse. They don't deserve to grow up too fast and not experience a childhood. They don't deserve what Jade and I had to go through. I can't and I won't. I knew when I first saw you freshman year you would be the hardest to get over and I still haven't gotten over you. I don't think I ever will.

"But you deserve a lot more than just someone who is going to have sex with you. You deserve a guy who's going to love you for the rest of your life and who's going to marry you. To have children

69

with. To treat you with respect and dignity and grace. Keep you on that pedestal where you most certainly belong. You deserve a guy who's going to wake up every day and say, 'Damn, I'm lucky because I'm with Ashlynn Miller.'"

Never taking my eyes off hers, I said, "That's what you deserve. Not me. Not this mess."

She closed her eyes and more tears fell from them. She tried to lean in for a kiss when I dropped my hands from her face. Her bottom lip was quivering when she looked up at me and said, "I still don't understand, Jason."

My blood pressure instantly raised and my heart beat accelerated. How could she not see why we couldn't be together? I couldn't do that to her. As much as I wanted her and needed her in my life as something much more than a friend, I had to push her away.

Does she think that little of herself that what I said doesn't matter to her? I'm not worth it.

"What don't you understand, Ash? Do you not understand that I'm a horrible mess of a person? Do you not understand that I would fuck this up?"

I took a minute to catch my breath and attempted to calm down. I began to pace back and forth because I didn't know what to do or say. Collecting my bearings, I said, "I just told you those things so you would understand why we can never be together."

I slammed my hand against the wal,l which in turn made her jump a little. *Good, she needs to be scared.* She needed a rude awakening and to realize she deserves much more than what I can offer her.

"I mean, *dammit*, Ash! You're beautiful and sweet and pure. Me, on the other hand, I'm a fuck up and a mess. I don't deserve you. And I will not put myself in a situation where I hurt someone the way my dad hurt my mom and his children. Especially with you."

She gasped and placed a hand to her beautiful chest. Scrunching her eyebrows together, Ash whispered, "You think I'm beautiful and you think you're a mess?"

I just shrugged my shoulders in defeat and shook my head. "I don't think that, Ash. It's a fact and I'm just pointing the obvious out to you."

She took her lower lip into her mouth and bit down on it. She had this far off look on her face like she was thinking about something and then this sweet, innocent smile came across her beautiful face.

Ash let go of her bottom lip and walked over to me, placing a hand on either side of my face. Never taking her eyes off me, she whispered, "Do you know what we make, Jason?" Not allowing me to answer she said, "We even each other out, because together we make a beautiful mess."

It was in that moment I was awakened. I was given a second chance and I knew exactly what I wanted, Ashlynn Miller, and I was never going to let her go again.

Sucking in a breath, I felt tears forming in my eyes. I couldn't believe the words that left Ash's beautiful lips. Leave it to her to see the good in such a fucked up situation. I laughed and then looked into her caramel colored twinkling eyes and said, "Yeah, I guess we do."

***

The rest of Spring Break was indescribable. We had the time of our lives together getting to know one another. Of course there were a few stolen kisses but nothing more because I wanted to take what we had going on as slow as possible. I wanted to enjoy it and I wanted to make this work because I knew with all my gut I wanted Ashlynn for a long time.

Eternity.

We splashed around in the water, tanned in the hot sun, and I was even lucky enough to rub sun tan lotion all over Ash's beautiful body. It was actually funny because during our time on the beach I was cooling off in the water and Ashlynn was tanning while reading a book when a guy our age walked up to her. I wanted to punch the little shit right in the face but I slowly made my way up to where our things were laid out, never taking my eyes off Ashlynn.

The second she saw me, I swear there was a twinkle in her eye and right as the guy was getting ready to ask her out, she got up and jumped right into my arms, wrapping her legs around me. It took me by surprise but I quickly welcomed it and wrapped my arms around her and grabbed ahold of her ass and gave it a squeeze. She squealed and then bit my lower lip and begged for entrance.

I happily obliged because I am a red blooded American male and when you have a gorgeous girl licking and nipping your lip you will do just about anything for that girl. I know I would for Ashlynn. We were both moaning into each other's mouths when she pulled back and said, "I think he's gone."

I pretended to look around and then looked back at her and said, "I don't think he is."

What came out of her mouth was this beautiful giggle and then she said, "You know what? I don't think he is, either. You think we could do better?"

I squeezed her butt cheeks and pulled her even closer to me where she could feel my hard-on and said, "Most definitely."

While we were having fun being with one another and getting to explore one another, we hadn't actually defined our "relationship." But I knew we weren't going to see other people. Boy, was I damn proud of that. To finally say that Ash was mine was ... incredible.

***

Tonight was our last night in Florida and tomorrow we would go back to "normal." Whatever the word normal is. To some people normal is ordering caviar and drinking champagne every damn day and still wanting more. To some normal is selling your body for money. To some normal is lying, manipulating, and cheating. But to me normal is what I have right now ... Ashlynn by my side and my secret out in the open.

I had decided to make Ashlynn and myself a candlelit dinner out on the patio. Cooking is a secret passion of mine; one that not a lot of people know about. It's kind of funny actually, because looking at me you would never guess that I, Jason Steven Williams, am a great cook. Any chance I could get, I watched the *Food Network* channel.

For dinner I had made grilled shrimp tacos with a tangy sauce and dirty rice. I also opened one of my dad's many red wines that would go perfectly with our dinner. I was mixing up the rice when Ashlynn walked in wearing this beautiful sundress that instantly took my breath away. She walked over and wrapped her arms around my middle and kissed my chest. I dropped the spoon I was holding and wrapped my arms around her and we just stood there, breathing one another in.

At the same time I looked down at her, Ash looked up at me. I kissed her on the forehead and said, "You look beautiful."

This beautiful blush came across her face. "And you look like a mess."

She began to back away and I just laughed and pulled her back to me. She giggled and wrapped her arms around me. I moved in and whispered against her lips, "You're the beautiful to my mess."

I then kissed her on the lips. "How can I help?"

I told her to fill us up each a glass of wine and wait out on the patio. She happily obliged and poured us each a glass and took a healthy sip. I walked over to her. "Can I have a taste?" She began to hand me my glass when I wrapped her in my arms and my mouth was instantly on hers and I was sweeping my tongue in her mouth. She tasted of sweet red wine with a bit of tang and Ashlynn.

I started to wonder what other parts of her would taste like but this had to go slow. Impossibly slow because I didn't want to mess it up, so as much as I didn't want to, I set her back down and she smiled up at me. "How did you like the wine?"

I couldn't help it so I kissed her again and said, "Insatiable."

She tried to deepen the kiss but I put her at arm's length and said, "If you don't go out there right now I'm going to carry you back to my room. And Ash? I'm trying really damn hard not to right now."

She just nodded and took a few steps backwards from me. Picking up the wine glasses, she started to walk out to the patio but stopped and turned. "I'll be waiting for you."

The second she walked out, I began to set up our plates but my phone started to ring. I picked it up and saw that it was an Unknown caller, so I pressed the Ignore button.

Getting everything situated, I started to pick up our plates but my phone started to ring again. I saw that it was Unknown again but I picked it up anyway. "Hello?"

As soon as I heard the man's voice, I automatically knew who it was. Of course I hadn't talked to him since Jade and I left for school but you never forget your dad's voice. "Jason. We need to talk."

Chapter 6

Ashlynn

I couldn't believe what Jason had told me about his and Jade's childhoods. It completely broke my heart. No wonder he was questioning us becoming a couple because first he had to trust somebody completely in order to tell them about what he called his mess. I also couldn't believe what his parents had done to him and Jade.

To be perfectly honest, I wasn't really sure which parent was worse. Their dad for degrading them and beating the shit out of Jason or their mom for looking the other way. Either way, I think they both deserved to burn in hell for what they did to their children and how they ruined their lives.

He had to open up his heart, and while a part of me was grateful he had chosen to tell me, another part was terrified completely because I didn't want to think about what struggles we would have to go through.

I've read so many books where the struggles are completely worth it in the end and with Jason I have to agree. In my heart and my mind I knew that we would go through struggles and heartbreaks and this would be a complete mess. I knew there would be tears shed and shouts and screams from either end. I knew there would be words said we would later regret.

But without a doubt in my body I also knew there would be beauty, laughter, joy, and most importantly love shared between the two of us. I just didn't know about all the struggles we were going to face until the last night we were in Florida.

Everything seemed to be going amazingly between Jason and me. However, as I waited for him out on the deck for our dinner, I noticed him on the phone and that's when his whole demeanor shifted and the mess we would have to face began. He walked out onto the deck, and while we ate dinner, I didn't taste a thing. It all tasted like cardboard because in the pit of my stomach I knew something was horribly wrong. I wanted to ask him about it but I knew that with Jason I had to give him his time. I knew that if I pushed him too far he would close off from me completely and indefinitely. So I gave him his time … two months to be exact.

***

"I still can't believe you haven't spoken to Jason since you guys got back from Spring Break,"

Derrick said while rubbing some suntan lotion on his face.

Derrick, Patrick, Sarah, and I decided to go to the beach for the day. While it sucked that we hadn't seen Jason since Spring Break ended, we also hadn't seen much of Jade, either. Even though Jade and I lived together, she was always closed off in her room or over at Jason's. While it hurt, I had to think that maybe something was going on at home and they didn't want to talk about it.

Hell, Jade never even told me how awful their childhoods were. I would be lying if I said that it didn't hurt, because it hurt like a complete bitch. I had never gone through something like that; not even along the same curvy, twisted lines, so I can only imagine what it would feel like peeling that bandage off and opening up the wound.

I looked over at Derrick and just gave a shrug of my shoulders. "What am I supposed to do? I've tried to text Jason and I've tried to talk to Jade but they're so closed off."

This whole thing is just so jumbled up and I don't know what to do or what I'm supposed to say to anybody. That is, if I'm supposed to say anything in the first place. Jason told me the secrets that were buried deep inside his closet, Jade hasn't told me anything, and Derrick, Patrick, Isabelle, Ryder, Sarah, and Gabe all just think that Jason is being a pussy and they don't know what's going on with Jade.

However, I can't explain to them what exactly is going on. So in cases like the one I'm in right now I just shrug my shoulders, hoping maybe that'll be

*enough of an answer ... but for how long exactly?
I'm not so sure.*

I looked down at my twisted fingers when I felt an arm wrap around me and I turned to see Sarah looking at me, giving a sympathetic smile. Sarah and Gabe were like the parents of the group. While we are all going through our relationship drama now, they went through theirs back in high school. I was jealous of that but like every relationship, there are good and bad times and I'm just having to go through the bad times right now.

"OMG. Hot ass at two o' clock!" Sarah and I turned to Patrick and he was pointing behind Sarah and I. So as not to make it completely obvious, we turned around all the way and recognized that it was the guy from when Isabelle and I went Christmas shopping together.

We turned back around and saw Patrick fanning himself, saying, "Hot damn, he's gorgeous. I would just like to lick…"

That's when Derrick had begun to cough and said, "Yes, sweetie, what would you like to lick of his?"

Patrick's eyes got huge and he turned to Derrick and smiled. Ever so sweetly, he wrapped his arms around Derrick's neck and whispered, "They're just words, Derr, but the actions are what matter. So with that, Derrick … I love you," and Patrick kissed him on the lips.

If I had somebody by my side being able to do that, to I would *so* not hate Patrick and Derrick in this moment. Hell, I don't even hate them because they are so damn cute together. They even one another out because while Patrick is outspoken and loud, Derrick is quiet and reserved and you can tell from just one look they love each other quite a bit. In complete and total honesty … I'm jealous.

That's when Sarah had to say, "Well, I have to get going, chickies. Gabe and I have to make all the final touches before the wedding."

Right then and there I went from feeling like nothing to feeling like complete and utter shit. I hated bitching like that but it sucks when you know the person who you are going to spend the rest of your life with and you don't know how to fix the problems in his life. You have to watch from a distance because he won't let you in and as much as you try to help, he pushes you away.

After Sarah gave us each a hug she said, "The next time you guys will see me, I'll be Mrs. Gabe Prescott!"

We all laughed and cheered, but I couldn't help but wonder when it would be my time to say things like that. It just seemed like everyone around me was finding someone to spend the rest of their life with. Of course there was Jade, because I couldn't see her ever settling down. If she did, though, it would take someone who was out of this world because I didn't see her changing anytime soon.

Once Sarah packed up her beach bag and left, Patrick and Derrick decided to go play in the water, so I laid on my stomach, welcoming the peace and quiet and started to read.

Reading is the only thing that calms me and helps me escape. By reading it's almost like I'm torturing myself because I wouldn't have to read if my life wasn't such a fuck up right now.

I envy Isabelle because she's no longer reading books, but writing them about her and Ryder. While I probably would never write a book, I do look forward to the day where it's a possibility that I'll be able to share the beauty in life and not have to read about it in order to escape mine.

I was on the last chapter of my book when a little girl walked up to me and asked, "Do you know where my brother is?"

I sat up, looked at her, and saw that she wasn't much older than four. I put my book back in my bag and turned to her and said, "No, but I can help you find him. I'm Ashlynn, by the way. What's your name, sweetie?"

She gave a tiny smile and said, "Jacquelyn."

I placed my hand out to shake her hand and asked, "What's your brother's name, Jacquelyn?"

We started our walk around the beach when she said, "Neil."

I was about to ask that sweet little girl what her brother Neil looked like when we hear a deep male voice screaming, "Jacquelyn! Jacquelyn! Jacquelyn!"

We turned around and saw a guy running all over the place carrying a little boy, and then Jacquelyn screamed, "Neil! Tommy!" The guy stopped in his tracks to face us and saw his little sister. The biggest smile came across his face and he began to run to her.

Releasing her hand from mine, Jacquelyn scurried on over to her big brother.

After he picked her up into his arms and spun her around, Neil placed her back in the sand and looked into her eyes. Very seriously he said, "Jack-O-Lantern, you can't run away like that again, okay? You had me really scared that something might happen to you."

That was when he turned to look at me and a little smile appeared on his face, but just as quickly he looked back at his little sister and said, "What if this nice lady wasn't here? I don't know what I would have done."

In a tiny little voice, Jacquelyn squeaked, "I'm sorry, Neil. I love you," and wrapped her arms around his neck and kissed him on the cheek. Just like that Neil melted and he changed from this scary big guy to this little softy right before my eyes.

I couldn't help but stare and smile. I said, "Well, I'm glad you found your brother, Jacquelyn." I prepared to leave but I heard Neil say, "Stay right here, Jacquelyn. Tommy."

Running towards me, Neil said, "Hey, wait up!"

I stop and turn around to see Neil running up to me smiling. He stops a few feet away from me and extends his hand and says, "Hey, I'm Neil."

I smiled and shook his hand. "I'm Ashlynn. It's nice to meet you, Neil."

When I said his name, his dimples appeared and a sly grin came across his face. He slowly let go of my hand. "You know it would be rude of me to not thank you properly for helping my little sister out; so would you want to go out to dinner with me sometime?"

I giggled. "Really? Is this how you pick up girls?" I looked over towards Jacquelyn and Tommy and asked, "Are those even your brother or sister?"

I looked back over at Neil. He had begun to laugh and then said, "That probably just looked really pathetic, but yes, they are my brother and sister. Truthfully, I just moved back here and don't really know anybody. Plus it kind of helps a little when your little sister finds some beautiful girl to help her out and find her dumbass brother because he can't watch two kids at a time."

All I could do was laugh because I wasn't expecting that and it kind of turned me on.

While Neil was blabbering, he looked down at the ground, but then he looked at me from under his eyelashes and asked, "So what do you think? Want to go out sometime?"

My stomach dropped and my heart began to beat really fast because while I wanted to say yes, I couldn't help but think about Jason because I knew when I first saw Jason and shook his hand, my heart belonged to him. Unfortunately, I couldn't wait forever, so against my better judgment and with slight hesitation I uttered, "Okay."

Neil quirked his head to the side and jokingly said, "Ash, you're going on a date with me. The least you could do is sound a little enthusiastic about it."

Giggling, I said, "I'll go out with you, Neil."

He smirked and said, "I don't believe you."

I giggled even harder. "I want to go out with you, Neil."

He laughed. "All right, Ash, relax."

I just rolled my eyes and pushed him playfully. "Does that work on everybody?"

In a serious tone, he said, "I don't know. I haven't done that with anyone, so you tell me?"

That's when I knew we had just went from playful to something else entirely. I was at a loss for words but my lips quirked up in a smile and I managed to say, "I'll let you know."

After Neil programmed my number into his cell, he said, "I'll text you what the plans are to go out."

I just nodded and said, "Okay." I started to walk away from Neil, Jacquelyn, and Tommy. I could feel Neil's eyes on me as I walked away and then my cell phone beeped. Taking it out of my pocket, I flipped it open. I saw a number I hadn't saved and read the message.

Unknown – Free Tonight?

I turned around and saw Neil looking at me with such intensity that I smiled. And before I could think about the huge mess that was going to cause, I quickly texted him back and winked. The second he looked down at his phone I turned around and walked back over to where Patrick and Derrick were sitting on beach towels, smiling and laughing.

Ashlynn – Pick me up at 8?

I was just about to sit down on my beach towel and soak in the sun for a little while longer when I got another text that said:

Neil – I'll be there!

Sitting down I texted him my address and just as I was about to put my phone away the beep went off, signaling that I had another text. I got giddy because I thought it was Neil. However, when I opened my phone I felt like I was going to have a panic attack because it said:

Jason – Can we talk?

Unbelievable! Just as I'm about to let go of Jason he comes back into my life and my world is turned upside down and I'm not sure what the right thing to do is.
After reading his text, Derrick nudged me and asked, "Sweetie?"

With just that one word the tears come pouring down my face and within seconds Derrick and Patrick were on either side of me, trying to calm me down and comfort me.

By the time I managed to tell them what had happened, I got two more messages; one from Neil and the other from Jason.

Neil – I can't wait for tonight.

Jason – Please Ash, I'm so sorry.

Taking my phone, Derrick asked, "What do you want to do, Ash?"

Looking down at the sand between my toes and taking a few deep breaths, I said, "I'm not sure."

Derrick just smiled and kissed me on the cheek. Moving away and looking into my eyes, he said, "I'm just going to give you my opinion on this. I know you still really like Jason but I think you should go on this date with Neil. From what you told me he seems like a really nice guy. Maybe it'll go somewhere, maybe it won't, but honey, you have to get out there and stop hiding behind your books."

Through a tearful smile, I said, "Thanks, Derrick. I love you."

Smiling, Derrick then kissed me on the forehead. "Always, babe. Now hop to it."

Once I wiped the tears from my eyes, I took a deep breath and sent out my replies.

Neil – I can't wait either

Jason - … no we can't. I'm attempting to move on, you should too.

As soon as my phone read, *Message Sent*, to Jason I felt somewhat relieved but I wasn't exactly sure what I was relieved about, to tell you the truth. Relieved because I said no to him or relieved because I knew that *this* wasn't over between him and I and that Jason would fight for us?

***

I decided on a pale blue sundress for my date with Neil along with some brown wedges. He said that he was taking me to a seafood restaurant that is out of this world spectacular. I was just about to close the door to my bedroom when the doorbell rang. I looked over to the clock and it read 7:50 and I became a little bundle of nerves.

I grabbed my purse from the couch and walked over to the door. Taking a deep breath to try and calm myself I opened the door and Neil was standing there looking downright fuckable. He had on these tan cargo shorts with a bright blue t-shirt that matched the color of his eyes. I looked up into his eyes and he looked like he was going to devour me. I bit my lower lip and then noticed he had an eyebrow ring.

Without thinking, I placed my finger to his eyebrow ring and said, "I didn't notice this earlier."

I looked into his eyes and he smiled and grabbed that exact hand and said, "That would be because I didn't have it in earlier. You ready to go?"

I smiled, and after locking the door, I turned to see Neil still staring at me. My stomach started doing somersaults and I had begun to laugh. "What?"

He just shook his head and said, "You look beautiful, Ashlynn."

I could feel my cheeks beginning to blush and looked down at the pavement. "Thank you."

I felt a hand under my chin and before I knew it, I was looking at Neil and he smiled. "You shouldn't be embarrassed of that." It seemed like all I could do around Neil was smile. Taking my hand in his, we walked to his car and he opened the door for me, which I thought was really sweet. After closing the door, he walked over to the driver's side and got in and started the car up. On our way to the restaurant, we talked about the simple things. Our favorite shows we like to watch. Movies. Music we listen to.

Before I knew it, Neil was parking the car and we were walking in. He held the door open for me and after the hostess took us to our table and got our drink order, the conversation started up again. Neil told me about Jacquelyn and Tommy and how important they were to him. He told me that he had to move back home because of some family problems. I could tell he didn't want to get into it so I didn't ask any questions. I loved that he felt comfortable with me, but in all honesty I felt like what Neil and I had would turn into a great friendship and nothing more.

Once our food arrived there were a few minutes of silence while we dug into the delicious seafood. We cracked open the lobster and slathered it with butter, while the sips of ice cold beer brought the meal together.

I was just about to take a bite of the buttered lobster when I heard my cell phone beep, notifying me that I had a text message. I ignored it because it's rude to check messages on a date, but Neil must have noticed it too, because he said, "You can answer it, Ash. I don't mind."

I quickly apologized and unzipped my purse. Opening my phone, my heart stopped when I read the text.

Jason – I'll never move on, Ashlynn.

I didn't think I shut my phone that loudly but Neil commented and said, "Are you okay?"

I looked up at him and he seemed really sincere. I attempted to nod my head but Neil said, "What's his name?"

I didn't think it was okay to talk to Neil about this while we were on a date together but Neil said, "Look, Ashlynn, it's okay. I just wanted to get to know you and I've had a lot of fun tonight but I can tell from the way you were reading that message that you're taken. I'd still like to be friends at least."

I smiled and nodded my head in approval. "I'm so sorry, Neil. I've had a great time tonight, too."

He gave a small smile and took a sip of his beer. After swallowing, he pointed to my phone and said, "All right, let's hear the story."

Setting down my phone, I looked up at him and said, "It's a long story." At that exact moment, the waitress came over with our bill.

Before I could grab the bill, Neil had it in his hands and was pulling out his wallet to get his card. I wanted to protest but he looked up at me and said, "I got this. If you're up for it, how about you buy a case of beer and we can talk about it at my place? My roommate will probably be there, so you can get two guys' perspectives."

Just as Neil put the card in the holder and set it back on the table, I put my hand on top of his and smiled. "Do you know how amazing you are, Neil?"

He chuckled. "It's by choice."

Once the waitress came back with our receipt, we left the restaurant. Picking up a case of beer, Neil started the drive to his apartment. I noticed that we were in the same apartment complex as Jason and I started to get really nervous. Grabbing the beer from the back, Neil said, "Follow me."

I followed Neil and stopped and saw that his apartment read **3B** and my heart stopped.

I started to walk into the apartment and then I saw the back of his roommate's head and heard him say, "Back so soon, Neil?"

Neil just laughed and said, "Nah, she's here with me."

Just then Neil's roommate got up from the sofa, turned around, and his eyes bulged out of his head. "Ashlynn?"

I heard Neil placing the beer on the breakfast bar and out of the corner of my eye, I saw him turn to me with a confused look on his face.

Without taking my eyes off his roommate, I whispered, "Jason."

Chapter 7

Jason

The second I heard the words, "Jason. We need to talk," my heart dropped. Why did it have to be as soon as I put everything out on the table with Ashlynn? I felt like we had made a huge breakthrough and then this bastard has to call and ruin it, just like Jade's and my childhood.

I just didn't understand why he couldn't leave me alone and let me live my life. He never tried to talk to Jade, but it was probably because I threatened to kill him if ever hurt her with his words or his fists ever again. I knew it hurt Jade and that's why she never did relationships; well that and because of what had happened in high school.

The both of us were just two damaged souls and we needed people who were going to help us with the messes and mistakes we were bound to make. Luckily, I had found mine … Ashlynn. I just hoped that Jade would find hers.

Looking through the glass doors at the view of Ashlynn sitting out on the deck, I let out a deep breath and said, "All right," and quickly hung up before I could take back the single hardest word I have ever had to speak.

While it hurt to say goodbye to Ashlynn before we even got started, I knew that if I didn't hear my dad out, Ashlynn and I wouldn't last the long run and goddamn, I was in it for the long run with her.

Once Ashlynn and I got back from Florida, I closed off from her because I had to hear what my dad had to say to me and what he told me left me emotionless.

Picking up the phone to call my dad, my heart was beating so fast. I was about to hang up because it just kept ringing but then I heard the phone pick up and my dad say, "Jason?"

I quickly gulped down my nerves and said, "What is it you wanted to talk about?"

Mom and Dad were still together but they both deserved one another because they were two of the most horrible human beings I had ever come in contact with and the fact that both their blood ran through mine and Jade's veins disgusted me beyond belief.

I heard some heavy wheezing on the other end and then I heard, "I'm dying."

I didn't know what to say to that, because if he wanted my sympathy, he sure as hell was looking in the wrong spot. In fact, I was the last person he should be asking sympathy from … besides Jade.

I didn't say anything so he went on.

"I have Stage 4 liver cancer and I'm not going to last much longer. I um—"

I thought the line disconnected, so I took the phone from my ear to look but I saw that he was still on the other end. I closed my eyes and said, "Are you still there?"

I heard him choking up and he said, "Yeah, I'm still here. I, um, I don't even know what to say for the things I have done to you and Jade. Sorry doesn't even come close and I wanted to ask for your forgiveness."

I just started laughing. "Really? You're asking for forgiveness now because you're dying? You will never get my forgiveness and if you so much as contact Jade I will shoot you where you stand. You hear me? You made your choices and I hope you rot in hell for what you did to us. I just can't believe I let you and Mom get to me like this.

"You don't even deserve to hear this but I met this girl and I want to spend the rest of my life with her. But you know what I think about when it comes to her? The fact that I'm scared out of my goddamn mind to end up like you. She means way too fucking much to me. I just don't understand how some bastard could treat his wife and kids like the way you treated Mom, Jade, and I."

Slamming my fist into the wall of my apartment, I yelled, "FUCK! That bitch doesn't even deserve me standing up for her because she fucking watched what you did to us!"

I tried to calm myself down so I went to the refrigerator and pulled out an ice cold beer and took down half of it in one gulp. Slamming the bottle down, I waited to hear what else he had to say.

All I heard for a good minute was heavy wheezing but then he said, "I've wanted to apologize for a long fucking time now, Jason. You have no idea how I feel about the way I treated you and Jade, but especially you. You were my punching bag for so many years, but the reason I'm asking you to forgive me is because I know that eventually you will. And I can say this because I know it's the truth ... you will forgive me because you are nothing like me. You are so much more. So much better than me. Than I ever will be.

"I can't say that I don't think I deserve what's happening to me because I know I do. I think it took Stage 4 liver cancer to finally call you because there hasn't been a day where I haven't wanted to pick up that phone and call you and do something so simple, yet so difficult as apologize for my actions and my betrayal. By blood I am your father, but I haven't been your father in a long fucking time. Probably since you and Jade were four, if that. But I'm asking if you'll give me a chance to prove myself to you guys."

Through the process of his speech I went from complete rage to sympathy for this man. It's sad that when something difficult happens that's what it takes for some people to own up to their actions. To apologize for what they've done to those around them.

I was getting ready to say something and I'm not sure what exactly, but he said, "I'll be here when you want to talk. If you want to talk," and with that the line went dead and I was left speechless.

I knew I had to get it over with, so I called Jade and told her I would pick her up in fifteen minutes. She could tell something was wrong because she wasn't her witty self. She was actually acting like when we both lived at home. She was scared and timid and shaking.

Getting back to my apartment, I told Jade to sit down on the sofa while I went to get us some beers. Walking back over to the sofa, I handed one to Jade, and with shaky fingers she gripped the bottle and took a huge gulp.

Wiping the excess beer from the corners of her mouth, she looked up at , and with tears in her eyes, she said, "What's the matter, Jason?"

Now it was my turn to take a gulp of my beer. I couldn't look into her eyes when I uttered the one single word I would forever hate. "Dad." I heard her take a huge deep breath and then I turned to her and wrapped her up in my arms and tried to calm her down.

I hated myself for having to tell her because I knew she would just crumble. I knew it was going to be harder on her because while growing up, I was the one getting hit; all she could do was stand there and watch as our father beat the living fuck out of me and then try and bandage me up afterwards. I could only imagine how small she felt, but I made a promise to myself a long time ago, one that I am unwilling to break, that I would protect my sister till I take my last breath.

After what seemed like forever, Jade broke away from my arms and went to the bathroom to probably get some tissues. I just sat there on the sofa and slowly took sips of my beer because I didn't know what else to do.

I was just about to ask Jade if she was okay when she walked out into the living room and sat down. "Please don't be mad at me when I say this, but I want to see him."

Taking a sip of my beer, I placed it on the end table and then took her hands in mine. Looking up at her, my heart began to break because her nose was red, her eyes were puffy, and her bottom lip was quivering. I kissed my little sister, by four minutes, on the forehead and said, "I'll be there for support, but that's all."

She attempted to give a small smile, but who could honestly smile at a time like this? Instead she wrapped her arms around my neck and said, "I love you, Jason."

The rest of the school year seemed to go by in a complete blur for both Jade and I. I felt like it was a routine for me. I would get up, go to class, and act like I was paying attention and then come home and either drink myself to sleep or Jade and I would talk. While that last month of school was torture, there was also light in the darkness because it brought Jade and I closer together as siblings but it pushed Ashlynn and I further away from each other as far as becoming a couple.

Once our junior year of college ended, both Jade and I packed up a week's supply of clothes and went back to our hometown to visit our dad and talk to him. I wish I could say that our visit was pleasant, but it isn't pleasant when you visit someone who you have hated all of your life and they're apologizing solely because they're dying.

What I can say is that there were many tears shed and apologies made, but no forgiveness or peace was made. All I know is that from the conversation my father and I had earlier on the telephone it showed that I'm not such a mess and that I can't be with Ashlynn. I just hope that she hasn't given up on us yet.

More importantly ... on me.

***

"Hey, thanks again for the extra room. It's like a miracle I found a place to live on such short notice."

My new roommate's name was Neil James. He told me that he'd moved back to help with his family and apparently there were some issues going on but I could tell that it was close to home ... literally. I totally got where the dude was coming from because I didn't want to talk about my family issues either, so whether he knew it or not, we shared a common bond.

I slapped him on the back and said, "Don't sweat it, Neil. It's nice to have a roommate because it gets kind of lonely around here sometimes."

Neil and I had just finished moving him into the apartment for the day. We both thought it would take a lot longer than three hours but it was still the afternoon. I decided to just relax for a Saturday night and maybe grow some balls and text Ashlynn.

I know what you guys are thinking. That I haven't seen Ashlynn in a month or two and I don't even have the decency to call her, but I was scared shitless of her rejection and I didn't want to hear the words come from her beautiful mouth. I didn't want to hear a sentence that formed, "I can't, Jason."

I decided to grab a beer from the fridge and just veg out in front of the television for a while. Neil plopped down next to me with a beer in hand and said, "Well, I'm going to take my little brother and sister to the beach. You can come if you want."

I just smiled and said, "Thanks, but I'm just not in the mood for it today. Maybe some other time."

Neil just slapped me on the back and said, "Well, okay, then," and walked back to his room.

I didn't take my eyes off the television when he came out of his room and headed to the door but then he said, "When I come home, we're talking about the girl on your mind, Jas," and with that he left the apartment. It gave me time to be filled with my sorrows.

I'm not sure exactly how many pep talks I had to give myself to finally text Ash, but I did, twice, and I can't say that I blame her for saying:

Ashlynn – … no we can't. I'm attempting to move on, you should too.

A half hour later, Neil came back from the beach and told me all about this gorgeous girl he met and that he was taking her out on a date tonight. I was happy for him because at least one of us was living his life. After Neil got ready, he came out to the living room and had a beer with me.

"Well, wish me luck. I feel lucky about this one."

I laughed and said, "How lucky?"

He just smirked and said, "That's for me to know, but she seems like a special one."

A few hours later and a few more beers in my system, I texted her again and just told her the truth.

Jason – I'll never move on, Ashlynn.

I was waiting for her to text back when I heard the front door unlock and open. "Back so soon, Neil?"

Neil just laughed and said, "Nah, she's here with me."

I wanted to see the beautiful girl Neil met at the beach and took out for a date when I saw blonde hair and bright blue eyes staring at me. "Ashlynn?"

I thought she was going to collapse because she barely whispered my name. "Jason."

I couldn't believe that Neil was talking about Ashlynn and I felt like someone kicked me in the balls because I couldn't breathe. I looked over at Neil and he looked between me and Ashlynn and then I saw him put everything together.

He looked over at me. "This is her." It was more of a statement than a question because he could see our reactions with his own eyes.

He then looked over at Ashlynn and said, "This is him."

What the fuck does he mean by that? Were they talking about me on their date? And if they were, then why was Neil bringing her back to our apartment? My blood instantly boiled and I slammed the beer I was holding onto the end table and staggered on over to Ashlynn.

She looked terrified out of her mind and walked backwards to the front door.

I was just about to reach out to her when Neil pushed me away. "Dude, you need to calm down."

With words like that I completely lost it and shoved Neil away. "Fuck off, Neil. You need to stay out of this."

Neil managed to get ahold of me from behind. "It's not what you think, Jason. You need to calm down and I'll explain all of it to you, okay? But dude, you seriously need to calm the fuck down. Look at Ashlynn. You're scaring the hell out of her."

With a shrug, Neil let go of me and I looked over in Ashlynn's direction. Tears were falling down her face. I wanted to wipe them away but it felt like she fucking ripped my heart out of my chest and stomped all over it. I just couldn't deal with the dad issues and then to top it all off with a cherry, my girl walking in with my roommate. What the fuck was I supposed to think?

So I walked over to her and as calmly as I could, I bit out the words, "I shared something so personal with you and you just fucking ripped my heart out. I thought you were different, Ashlynn, but I was so wrong about you. So incredibly fucking wrong."

The second the words left my mouth, I wanted to fall to my knees and apologize, but I didn't have time, because she turned her back to me and swung the front door open and ran.

I just stood there until I was shoved out of the way by Neil, who didn't even look back at me when he said, "We're going to have a *long* fucking talk when I get back."

By the time I walked over to the sofa and sat down, I was crying. I cried because I'd fucked this all up again. I cried because I made this mess when it wasn't even necessary. I cried because of the words I said to Ashlynn when I didn't mean a damn one. I cried because I just hoped that she'll have it in that huge heart of hers to forgive me yet again for being such a huge ass mess.

I didn't even hear the door open and close when Neil walked over and sat in a chair, looked at me and said, "Well, let's start from the beginning then, Jason."

He told me about how he met Ashlynn this afternoon at the beach and how he really liked her. He told me about how when they were at the restaurant they had a great time, but he could feel they were just going to be friends. He told me about how he could sense she wasn't over someone and then she got a text. He then told me that he offered to let her vent to him about it over a couple of beers and she accepted.

"Honestly, man, I had no idea that Ashlynn was the girl, but what the fuck was that all about with you? How could you treat her like that? Because I could tell you from the way she saw your text at the restaurant she wasn't over you. That was the first time since I met her that her eyes glistened and glittered and it looked like she was really alive for the first time and taking her first breath. And in a matter of, oh I don't know, two minutes of you seeing her, you took it all away."

Taking a huge breath, I looked over at Neil and told him everything. I told him about my childhood and I told him about how my dad is dying. I told him about how the first time I laid eyes on Ashlynn I knew she was the one. The one who would save me. The one who would help me out of the mess I'm in. And in a dream world, the one I would marry. But now that I've talked to my dad, the one I am positive without an ounce of question I will marry someday.

By the time I finished, Neil got up from the chair and walked over to the fridge and grabbed two beers. Popping the tops off, he walked back over and handed me one and then sat down and took a huge gulp of his. and said, "Well, fuck me, Jason." He took another gulp. "You've got a lot of groveling and apologizing to do to make it up to Ashlynn. You know that, right?"

Now it was my turn to take a huge gulp of my beer. Struggling to swallow, I said, "Yeah, got any advice?"

He gave a low laugh and said, "Help on fixing the mess you're in? Fuck, no! I've got my own problems to deal with. I don't need to add a chick into that because well, it would be a big mistake on my end and hers."

I just laughed and said, "Thanks for the advice, Neil."

He got up out of the chair and slapped me on the back. "Anytime, Jas," and began to walk back to his room to let me have some peace and quiet to try and figure out how what I was going to do. Right before he closed his door he said, "Good luck with that mess, Jason."

I just nodded my head and said, "Thanks. I'll definitely need it."

Chapter 8

Ashlynn

Neil was nice enough to drive me home and the whole ride was filled with complete silence, besides my sniffling. By the time he parked the car, I had somehow managed to stop crying but just before I got out of the car, Neil said, "I don't know what's going on between you and Jason, but I know from the way he looked at you that he really cares about you. I know you just met me today but please don't give up on him."

I turned and gave Neil a kiss on the cheek and said, "Thanks, Neil."

He smiled and nodded his head. "Anytime, Ashlynn. I'm here if you ever need to talk or anything."

After nodding my head, I closed the door and waved goodbye to him.

Letting myself into my apartment, I was grateful that Jade wasn't there because I just needed my alone time to think about what in the hell was the right decision to make with Jason. I decided to take a long hot bubble bath to release the tension and calm down. I brought my Kindle in there with me to relax but I couldn't even read, that's how bad I was hurting.

After an hour of dozing on and off in the tub, I dried myself off with a towel and changed into a t-shirt and panties and climbed into bed. I tossed and turned for what seemed like forever. All of a sudden I heard rain pitter patter against the window with the wind blowing the trees back and forth. I loved listening to the sound of the rain, but the thunder slowly erupted and shuddered.

Thunderstorms are actually my favorite time. I love reading a book and cuddling up by the fireplace. That was my source of peace and tranquility, but right now in this moment I feel restless. My brain was running a mile a minute because I was questioning everything that had happened between me and Jason. He showed me a piece of him that he hadn't told anyone else about and then he ran away. I realized that he was testing me and I failed.

I proved him right ... that nobody stays.

I was so scared of getting hurt that I didn't open my eyes and my mind ... but most importantly my heart, to the possibilities of feeling happy and alive.

My eyelids were starting to get heavy when there was a loud pounding coming from the door. I immediately jumped out of bed and my heart started thumping. I looked over at the clock and it read 12:30 a.m. I wondered who it was. Before I walked out of my bedroom, I bent down and pulled on some sweatpants.

Walking out into the living room, I heard another knock at the front door. I unlocked the latch. I then took a deep breath and placed my hand on the knob and turned. The door was only halfway open when I saw Jason.

He was standing there, all disheveled and staring at me, but looking as beautiful as ever. I took a second to drink him in. The rain drenched his blond wavy hair, plastering it to his face. His eyes were boring into mine. I felt like they were looking deep into my soul. I watched as Jason breathed out, his chest rose and fell as the warm air left his lungs. He clenched his fists together and moved his weight from one foot to the other. It seemed as if he were nervous; he sucked his lower lip into his mouth and his eyebrows scrunched together.

I tilted my head and studied him. "What do you want, Jason?"

Dropping his head to look at the pavement, he placed his hands on his hips and let out a low laugh. Seconds went by and then his eyes met mine and he cupped my face in his hands. His thumbs moved back and forth along my cheeks to soothe me and then he whispered, "It's not what I want, Ash, it's more like who. It's you. Ashlynn, I want you." He huffed and said, "I love you."

He then crushed his mouth to mine and I wrapped my arms around his neck. We were standing in the doorway of my apartment but Jason lifted me in his arms and walked in, closing the front door behind him.

Jason set me down on the floor and we both just stared at one another. We were both breathing pretty heavily and neither of us knew what to do.

Jason started to step back from me, never taking his eyes off me but I said, "Take the jacket off, Jason."

He tilted his head but did as I said and just as he was about to set it on a nearby dining room chair, I took fistfuls of his shirt in my hands and crashed my mouth to his. He wrapped his arms around my waist and lifted me so my feet were dangling from the floor. I wrapped my arms around him and held on for dear life, hoping he wouldn't push me away again and say, "I can't." He started to kiss my neck as he walked us back to my room and my heart was beating wildly out of my chest.

Not from nerves, but from pure excitement.

He laid me down on the bed and came on with me. The weight of his body on top of mine was comfortable. His lips on mine were everything I ever expected in a kiss … Jason's kiss. His hands on my body left goose bumps where they previously touched and butterflies fluttering in my stomach.

Jason sucked my lower lip into his mouth and bit down a little. He trailed his hands up and down my body and then stopped at the bottom of my shirt. Moving his head back to look at me, his eyebrows scrunched together. The look in his eyes was so sincere and he looked almost nervous.

He was breathing heavily and managed to whisper, "Ash?"

I let out a breath and nodded my head. "I want you, Jason. I've always wanted you."

He kissed me again on the lips and then took my shirt off and gasped when he realized I wasn't wearing a bra. His eyes got huge and he licked his lips and then looked back at me. The look in his eyes completely turned me on and before I could say anything, he was sucking one of my nipples into his mouth. I gasped, and before I knew it, Jason was releasing my nipple and looking at me.

My mouth dropped open and before I could stop myself, I said, "Why'd you stop?"

Jason leaned down and kissed me on the lips and then just started chuckling. He bit his lip and said, "I knew you would taste amazing. So sweet."

Before I could form words, his mouth was back on my nipple and he was pinching and rolling the other one with his hand. After a loud *pop* he moved to the other nipple and gave it the same affection and attention. The way he was sucking my nipples into his mouth and nibbling down, I thought I was going to come just like that.

Of course I had read about that in books but I never thought it was possible until now. I started to grind the lower half of my body up against him. We timed it perfectly; as hard as he sucked on my nipple, that's how hard I ground against him. Before I knew it I felt a zap run through me and I clenched my legs around him. I had ever experienced anything like that before. It was a mind-blowing, life-altering, phenomenal orgasm and I couldn't wait for Jason to be inside of me.

He started to suck on my neck while I got my breathing back to normal and then he moved up my body. "I knew you would be amazing. I just never thought I would be the one giving you this."

Smiling at me, Jason then moved down my body and began to trail kisses down my stomach and stopped at my belly button and licked it. I had my belly button pierced; he took the ring in his mouth and pulled away, which gave a little bit of pressure but it was pleasurable.

He then got on his knees and looked at me. "God, you're beautiful, Ash."

His hands were at my pants and a small smile came to my lips because I could feel his hands shaking. I lifted my hips to give him the answer to the question he was too afraid to ask but I knew was on his lips as well as his mind.

He began to pull just my pants down when I put my hands on top of his and said, "Both, Jason." He looked into my eyes and then put his thumb in the tops of my panties and began to pull them down as well. He was pulling them down so slowly and it caused me to get goose bumps and shake a little.

Jason instantaneously stopped what he was doing but I said, "Keep going, Jason."

As soon as they were off and falling onto the floor, he looked at me. "Ash, we don't have to—"

I cut him off right there and sat up and cupped his face in my hands. Without taking my eyes off hi,s I said, "Yes, we do. I mean, I want to. Do you?"

He put his hands on top of mine and said, "You don't even need to ask. You're the only girl I've wanted, Ash. You always will be."

His lips were again on mine and he was pushing me back so I was lying down on the bed. He gave little light kisses and then I realized that Jason was still fully clothed. I brought my hands to the bottom of his shirt and started to pull it up. He looked at me, realizing what I wanted, and helped me out. As soon as his shirt hit the floor, his mouth was on mine and I was rubbing my hands up and down his flat stomach and back, digging my fingernails into him.

He started to get up off the bed and put his hands to his jeans. Without taking his eyes off of me, he unbuttoned and then unzipped his jeans and pushed them off his hips. He left his boxers on and then climbed back on the bed.

Jason was just getting ready to kiss me when I asked, "Why'd you leave the boxers on?"

He looked at me and said, "I need a barrier, Ash. I want you, but not like this."

He started to lean into me when I placed my hands on his chest and said, "Jason, I don't care where it happens. For all I care it could be in an alley or in the backseat of a car. The only thing that matters is that it's with you."

He started to sit back on his knees and said, "Ash, it needs to be special."

I sat up on my knees and took his hands in mine and kissed them. "It will be. Simply because it's with you."

He took a sharp intake of breath and then said, "I don't even have—"

I cut him off and said, "I'm on birth control."

A couple of seconds went by and then he looked into my eyes. "Are you sure, Ash?"

I wrapped my arms around his neck, and right before I kissed him, I said, "Yes, Jason."

His lips were hesitant at first but then he wrapped me in his arms and laid me back down on the bed. We made out like two sex-starved teenagers for a while and then he lifted his head and began to kiss down my body. I got up on my elbows and looked at him and then he stopped at my mound. He didn't even have to ask because I moved my legs apart so he could get better access.

I saw him lick his lips and then he looked into my eyes and winked. I bit my lower lip and watched as he used his fingers to spread me apart and then licked my clit. My legs started to shake and Jason looked up at me and I nodded my head for him to continue.

He licked my clit up and down and before I could moan, he pushed a finger into me and moved it in and out. He moved his head away and said, "Fuck, Ash, you taste amazing." I just moaned because it felt so good. *I can definitely tell you it was ten times better than using my own fingers or my vibrator. Even though I was a virgin I still had sexual needs.*

Jason then sucked my clit into his mouth and pushed another finger inside me. He was hitting the right spot and just as I was about to come, he pushed another finger inside of me and I moaned his name over and over again as he pushed his fingers in and out of me.

I was still getting over my sexual high when Jason crawled up my body and looked at me and smiled. I instantly wrapped my arms around him and kissed him. I could still taste myself on him and I started to open my mouth when Jason's head moved back.

I looked at him and my eyebrows pushed together. He shook his head, then looked at me and said, "I'm sorry, Ash. I should have probably wiped my mouth. It's just I've never done that before. I'm sorry."

He was stuttering and apologizing and it was the most adorable thing. I just giggled because apparently while Jason did the deed, he hadn't done everything else. I sat up on my elbows and kissed him on the lips. "You've never done that before?"

Jason just shook his head back and forth and then looked at me. "The only girl I've ever wanted to do that to is you."

My stomach started doing somersaults and my heart started beating wildly. I wrapped my arms around his neck and pulled him down on top of me and kissed him. I sucked his lower lip into my mouth and heard him groan.I could feel his erection pushed up against his boxers and he was rubbing the lower half of his body up against me, causing a delicious friction but I needed more. So much more.

I couldn't take it anymore so I wrapped my legs around him and started pushing his boxers down his body with my feet. We were kissing but then Jason started to laugh against my mouth. He moved back and looked at me and said, "What have I done?"

I looked at him and said, "Besides give me an amazing orgasm with your mouth and fingers?"

With that question his pupils dilated and he jumped up off the bed and pushed his boxers down the rest of his body. His erection was up and ready for me and my eyes bulged out of my head because he was really big and I wondered if it would fit.

Jason must have been able to read my mind because as he crawled back on the bed he said, "Don't worry, Ash, I'll go slow." He got situated between my legs and I moved my legs further apart and lifted my hips to meet him. He placed one hand on the side of my face while the other was by my hips holding himself up. He leaned his head down and kissed me and started to push in.

I gasped because he was big but it wasn't painful; a little uncomfortable because I wasn't used to it, but not where I needed him to stop.

He was going really slowly but I looked into his eyes and said, "Jason." He stopped because he must have thought he was hurting me but I wrapped my arms around his neck and said, "Please." At the same time he lowered his head and his lips touched mine as he pushed all of the way in.

I had read in books and heard from friends that the first time it was really painful but this wasn't all that bad. It was a mix between pleasure and pain.

Jason stilled so I took the initiative and started to move. He moved his head back and tilted it and just laughed and then began to thrust in and out of me slowly but I said, "Harder, Jason."

Those two words were all it took because he moved out of me completely and then slammed right into me. All of the air left my lungs and I screamed his name. He thrust into me a few more times and I could feel his movements were becoming shaky and uneven.

I looked into his eyes and cupped his face in my hands and rubbed my thumb against his lower lip. He lowered his head and kissed my lips. "Ashlynn."

I looked into his eyes and smiled. He whispered, "I love you."

I could feel tears forming and then shakily I said, "I love you too, Jason."

We moved our bodies together a few more times and then Jason looked into my eyes and asked, "Ashlynn?"

I just nodded my head and he placed his thumb on my clit to apply a little pressure.

Before I could even predict it, something was overtaking my body and my pussy was clenching up around his cock. I felt him get harder and then I felt him come inside of me and then he collapsed on top of me. He was breathing heavily into my neck and I began to rub up and down his back.

We laid like that for a few minutes but then Jason slowly got out of me. I gasped, not because it hurt, but because I felt empty. He looked at me and the look in his eyes was scared.

I giggled and said, "I'm fine, Jason. I just … can't wait for next time."

I started to blush but Jason leaned down and kissed me on the cheek. "Neither can I, Ash. Neither can I."

I looked up at him and bit my lower lip and smiled. Jason winked at me and walked out of the room. He didn't say anything as he left but he didn't go far, because I heard the water in the bathroom going on and off. *Plus he was naked and holy hell! Jason Williams has a fine ass, a fine ass indeed.*

A couple of minutes later Jason walked back in with a wet washcloth and climbed up on the bed. I was laying the same way he left me but I started to bring my legs up to push them closer together out of pure embarrassment. Jason looked at me and lightly touched my legs; they instantly fell open to him.

He placed the warm washcloth down there and wiped me up and said, "I'm sorry."

I got up on my knees and wrapped my arms around him and said, "I'm not."

He moved back and looked into my eyes and shook his head back and forth. "I meant that I'm sorry for hurting you, Ashlynn. I'm not sorry for what we just did."

I gave a slight smile and then Jason started to get up off the bed. I unwrapped my arms from around him and watched him strut out of the room. Laying back down on the bed, I covered my naked self with a blanket.

Jason walked back into the room and then climbed in under the covers and pulled me to him. I wrapped a leg and an arm around him. Jason wrapped an arm around me and started rubbing up and down my back while his other arm was behind his head.

My head was on his chest and I looked up at him the same time he looked down at me and we both giggled. I smiled up at him and he asked, "Are you comfortable?"

I nodded. "Now I am."

He gave a light chuckle. "Yeah, I know what you mean."

Chapter 9

Jason

Turning over in bed, I couldn't believe the beautiful view in front of me. Ashlynn was laying on her side with her beautiful swollen lips puckered out, which of course only made me think of what the view would look like with her lips wrapped around my cock and her swallowing all of my cum when I came.

Anyway, her golden hair was flowing all over the pillow and the blanket was around her waist, which gave me the best view ever of her perky tits pushed together because of the way her hands were under her pillow. They were fully erect and just begging for me to suck on them, but I knew just having a taste of her tits wouldn't be enough and I knew that Ash would be sore. I still couldn't believe that Ashlynn gave me her virginity and I also couldn't believe that I told her I loved her.

I wasn't lying but I guess talking to my dad did some good because he showed me that I'm nothing like him and that I make my own choices in life. I will forever choose Ashlynn Paisley Miller to be in mine.

Ever so slowly I got up out of bed and put on my boxers and walked into the kitchen. Thankfully, Jade hadn't come home last night because it would have been rather awkward having to see Jade first thing in the morning after having sex with Ashlynn. *No, scratch that, because we didn't have sex. We made love.*

Rummaging through their fridge and freezer, I decided to make Ashlynn and I some waffles because I was starving from what she and I did last night. I pressed the coffee pot to make myself some coffee and then made Ashlynn some hot chocolate. I had everything set and ready to go. I was halfway to her room and I heard Ash waking up and making these little purring noises from stretching.

I just stood in the doorway with the breakfast tray and watched as she arched her back and her tits pushed up towards the ceiling, her hands were above her head. Her eyes were closed and her mouth was wide open, yawning, and my cock instantly got hard because of the way she looked. It reminded me of her coming to orgasm and a part of me just wanted to drop the breakfast tray and push my boxers down, jump up on the bed between her legs, and slide right inside her, but then I remembered cleaning her up with the washcloth and seeing the small amount of blood.

As much as I wanted my hard cock to be inside her tight wet pussy, I knew she would be sore for a few days, but of course we could always do things with my talented tongue and fingers. I started to think about that when I heard a beautiful girl clearing her throat and I looked over at Ash, who was up on her elbows with the blanket around her sexy, pierced bully button looking at me with a grin on her face. I swallowed and smiled and started to walk over to her bed.

I placed the breakfast tray in her lap and began to crawl on when Ash said, "Get naked, Jason."

I just laughed and in my best country accent, I said, "Why, yes, ma'am."

She just giggled and said, "We'll have to find you a cowboy hat, Sheriff Jason," and as soon as I stood up to take my boxers off, Ash saw how fucking hard I was and her eyes got huge. Then I saw her push the tray to the side and she licked her lips, never taking her eyes off my cock.

I started to get up onto the bed but Ash put her hand to my stomach and in this sexy, husky voice she said, "Stay there." She pushed the blanket off and got out of bed and then fell to her knees. Before I could comprehend what was going on, her mouth was on my cock. *Holy shit, could Ash give a blow job!*

She trailed her tongue along the bottom of my cock along that vein and my legs became wobbly. She must have noticed because she looked up at me from underneath her eyelashes and began to stand. Without taking her hand off my cock and the other off my balls, she deliriously pushed me to the wall and then sank down to the floor and sucked me all the way in. I knew I wasn't going to last long because I pre-came before my back was even up against the wall.

The tip of my cock hit the back of her throat and I thought she was going to gag but she didn't. She moved her mouth up and down and swirled her tongue along the tip, all the while gently squeezing my balls. I couldn't believe this girl because she was fucking amazing. Ashlynn really was this sexy ass librarian. She loved to read and was the smartest girl I knew but she also took control in the bedroom and gave a fucktastic blow job.

I could feel myself getting bigger in her mouth and I was becoming rigid. I knew without a shadow of a doubt I was going to come. I put my hand in her hair to push it out of the way because I needed to see myself come in her mouth and then I said, "Ash, I'm going to come."

I wanted to warn her in case she didn't want to swallow my cum, but she sucked me dry. She took down every creamy squirt I had and then for the love of all, she licked my cock clean and then licked her lips and kissed her way up to my lips.

She started to lean into my lips but I saw hesitation cross her face so I showed her what I wanted. I put a hand on either side of her face and crushed my mouth to hers. I tasted myself on her and I had thought it was going to be kind of disgusting but this was Ashlynn, and it made me think of just what exactly her talented mouth did wrapped around my cock.

I licked her lower lip and picked her up and walked her over to her bed but then remembered that damn breakfast tray was on her bed so I fell to the floor with her in my arms. She was breathless by the time she was lying on her back on the floor and she looked at me. I just winked and moved her legs open and said, "I'm hungry, too." Before she could say anything, I was sucking her clit into my mouth and pushing two fingers inside of her.

I couldn't believe how wet she was. Ashlynn wasn't wet, she was soaked. She was drenched. I knew she wouldn't last long, so I wanted to make this orgasm extremely strong. I sucked her clit harder into my mouth and rammed my two fingers in and out of her.

I felt her hands in my hair, squeezing and pulling and then she more or less screamed, "JASON!" I felt her tightening around my fingers, sucking them in, and then her orgasming. I pushed it out as long as it could go and then she just fell around me like a limp noodle.

I wiped my mouth across my hand and just laughed and moved up her body. I kissed first her lower lip and then her upper lip and said, "Good morning, Ashlynn."

Her eyes were still closed and this little smile came across her face. "Yes, it is."

I left her on the floor and got up and put the breakfast tray on her nightstand table. I then picked her up into my arms and placed her on the bed and sat behind her. Her back was to my front and she was still in a state of amazing orgasmic fucking bliss.

I picked up the hot chocolate and moved it underneath her nose. The second I did that she was up and ready. She greedily took the hot chocolate from me and took a huge sip. I was about to tell her to be careful because it might be hot but I realized it was probably room temperature by now.

Swallowing, she moaned and said, "Thank you."

I just smiled and kissed the back of her head while I wrapped my arms around her. She handed me back the cup and I traded the hot chocolate for the single plate of waffles.

She cut the waffles up in single bites and then lathered it up with maple syrup. I just laughed and asked, "Do you want some waffles with your syrup?"

She playfully nudged me and said, "Shh, I like syrup!"

She then took a bite of her waffle and upon swallowing turned sideways to me and I could see that she had some syrup on her face, along with a devilish grin. Ash leaned into me and I licked her maple syrup covered lips and then she sucked my tongue into her mouth and gently massaged it.

Releasing my tongue, I said, "Yeah, I think I love syrup, too."

She just giggled and turned around and went back to eating her waffles, occasionally sharing bites here and there with me while I drank my coffee and enjoyed the view.

Once we finished breakfast, I got dressed and told Ash that I had to go home but I would be back later. She just smiled and said, "Okay, I love you, Jason."

The words took my breath away and I couldn't believe that everything I would never have I was getting, and it was my choice. I was placing my shoes on when I stopped and leaned in and kissed her on the lips and said, "I love you too, Ashlynn, always."

She smiled against my mouth and I knew I had to leave soon or I would never leave.

I was just about to walk out of her room when I turned to her and she had this big smile on her face, staring at me. I winked at her and said, "So since I love you and everything, would you be my date to Sarah and Gabe's wedding?"

She just laughed and said, "Of course. You know, since I love you too and all." *I don't think I'll ever get used to hearing Ash say she loves me.* Walking over to her, I pecked her on the lips because anything more and I would be naked and inside her in two seconds flat.

I was just about to leave hers and Jade's apartment when I saw the front door open and Jade walked in.

She didn't see me but as soon as she closed the door and turned around, she said, "Oh hey, Jason. You're here early." But then she stopped and took in my appearance and must have noticed my hair was in disarray and my clothes weren't really in place, oh and the fact that I had a major hard-on, because she smiled and then said, "Fucking finally," and started to run towards me.

Or at least I thought, until she ran past me and screamed, "Ashlynn, you better be dressed when I run in there because I want to hear everything.

Okay, maybe not everything, but just say that the guy's name was henry or something besides, you know, my brother Jason! Oh this is so exciting!"

I just laughed and walked out the door down to my car and drove home.

Once I got home, I told Neil everything and he smiled. "I'm glad, Jason. I'm really happy for you guys because I've only known you for maybe a week and Ashlynn maybe 24 hours, but I could tell from just one look between the two of you that you guys are the real deal."

I patted him on the back and then decided to go take a shower.

I wanted to get back to Ashlynn as fast as possible but decided to give her and Jade time to talk, because Jade can certainly talk your ear off. I ended up just hanging out with Neil for the rest of the day, playing video games, eating pizza, and drinking beer. Before I knew it the clock read 10 p.m. and I had drank my fair share of beers with Neil, so I texted Ashlynn.

Jason – A little drunk right now so I'm going to stay here but I love you, Ashlynn Miller

In a matter of seconds I got a text back from Ashlynn saying:

Ashlynn – Be careful tonight. Jade and I will be packed and ready for you in the morning for the wedding! I love you, Jason Williams!

Smiling at my phone, I felt a pillow being thrown at my face and just started laughing. I looked over at Neil and he just laughed and said, "Oh my god, you're fucking whipped already, aren't you?" Without taking my eyes off the next text Ashlynn sent:

Ashlynn – Forever and always <3

I said, "Yeah, I am."

I heard Neil laughing but I just shrugged my shoulders and said, "One day, Neil, you're going to meet a girl who will completely flip your world upside down."

Without taking his eyes off the game we were playing on Xbox, he said, "Like I said before, Jason. Big mistake, in fact, huge." With a sly grin he looked over at me and said, "Like other places on my body."

We both laughed for a while and then I finished my beer and walked to the back of my room and closed the door. I quickly packed a bag for the wedding and then sent Ashlynn a text.

Jason – For eternity, love.

***

It only took an hour or two to drive to Sarah's house for the wedding, but it felt like years because Jade kept talking about how she was so excited for Ashlynn and I to finally get together. As much as I wanted her to shut her big ass yap, I was happy that my sister was acting like herself again and not moping around like before. Jade, Ashlynn, and I decided to stay at a local hotel. Sarah and Ryder offered to let us stay at one of their houses, but we declined. Ashlynn and I needed our privacy and Jade probably did too for after the wedding. Not that I wanted to know about my sister's sex life.

I had to carry everybody's bags to our rooms. Not that I minded carrying Ash's single bag, but Jade, of course, had to have a separate bag for shoes and clothes, and then one for hair and makeup. Like what the fuck were in those bags?

Once the door was closed to mine and Ashlynn's room, I asked, "Do you want to take a bath together?"

She just smiled and nodded her head.

I walked into the bathroom and turned the water to warm and filled it with a soap that was left next to the tub and watched as the soap quickly turned to bubbles. After the bath was filled, I walked out to our room and saw Ashlynn was talking to someone on the phone, smiling. I walked over to our bed and sat down and waited for her.

"Yes, Daddy. I know what you think but I'm really happy. Wait, you want to talk to him?" Ashlynn handed the phone to me and said, "My dad wants to talk to you." She then kissed me on the cheek and after sucking my earlobe into her mouth she whispered, "I'll be waiting for you."

Taking the phone from her, I gulped and said, "Hello?"

Her dad's voice came bellowing through and said, "Jason. Right?"

"Yes, Mr. Miller."

I heard him chuckle. "Well, at least you have manners. What do you want with my little girl, Jason Williams?"

I decided to just put it all out there. "To be perfectly honest, Mr. Miller, I want to marry Ashlynn Miller someday and I wanted to ask for your permission."

The line was silent for a second but then he said, "You're not kidding with me, are you?"

I shook my head but then realized he couldn't see me and said, "No, Mr. Miller. I'm not."

His tone then turned really serious and asked, "Why should I say yes to you, Jason?"

I let out a breath and said, "In complete honesty, Mr. Miller, you shouldn't. Ashlynn deserves everything and I can't give her that, but I can tell you that you'll never find anyone who loves your daughter as much as I do."

He laughed and said, "Well, you've got balls, kid. I'll give you that at least."

I cleared my throat and said, "Mr. Mill—" but was cut off when Ashlynn's dad said, "Call me Garrett, son."

I smiled and said, "Thanks, Garrett."

He just chuckled and said, "You know what? My little girl is very particular about who she lets in and I knew the second you both looked at one another she was yours. But I also know that you've got some problems, because I could tell from the look in your eye when you first saw my daughter you didn't want to have these types of feelings for her. I give you my blessing, but if you so much as cause my little girl any type of harm, I will kill you. You understand me, son?"

I just chuckled and said, "I'm sorry for laughing, Garrett, but you can't threaten me and then call me son. It kind of destroys the first thing you said."

I was kind of afraid for my life but then I heard him laugh and say, "I guess so. But I am serious on that threat, Jason."

I looked over to the bathroom and let out a breath. "I know you are, Garrett. I know you are."

"Well, great. I'll let you get back to whatever you and Ashlynn were doing. Talk to you soon, Jason."

I smiled and said, "Yeah, see you soon."

If he knew what I was getting into with Ashlynn, particularly inside of her, he would probably cut my balls off. Once I hung up the phone, I went and buried myself deep inside of Ashlynn and had her moaning and screaming my name.

***

"Are you sure I look okay?"

Ashlynn was fussing over the violet dress she was wearing for Sarah and Gabe's wedding reception. I unbuttoned the top three buttons of my long sleeve shirt and walked up behind Ashlynn, wrapping my arms around her.

Just before I kissed her on the side of her neck, I whispered, "You look beautiful."

I looked at her in the mirror and could see a blush coming across her beautiful face and chuckled. Turning around in my arms, Ash whispered against my lips, "Don't laugh at me," which only made me laugh more.

"Ashlynn, I'm not laughing at you. I just find it downright sexy that I can make a blush come across your beautiful face. Of course, it makes me think of me getting you to orgasm."

I didn't know if Ashlynn would hate me talking to her like that, because during sex I talked dirty in order to get off while picturing Ash, but with Ashlynn I would fucking love it beyond belief. I looked down at her and saw her biting her lip, and then she looked up at me and she had a look of sex.

Downright, bent-over, dirty, sweaty fucking.

She then smiled and leaned in and said, "Well, you can make me orgasm all night tonight if you want?"

She said it like a question which I was surprised about and I pulled her closer so she could feel my hard cock up against her. I knew the second she felt my hard-on because she gasped and I said, "Ashlynn, I always want, with you."

Before kissing me she wrapped her arms around my neck, twined her fingers within my hair and said, "Well, I guess we have that settled, then."

Leaning away, I smiled down at her and said, "Yeah, we fucking do."

Chapter 10

Ashlynn

I couldn't believe how quickly everything had changed for Jason and I, but a part of me deep down still wondered why he ignored me for a month and a half and I knew I would have to question him on it sooner rather than later. I also wanted to ask Jason what he talked to my dad about but I figured he would tell me when he was ready along with everything else going on in his life.

Waking up the next morning after Jason and I first made love was indescribable. At first I thought he left but then I smelled breakfast cooking and knew that it wasn't just a one-time thing between us. Even though we both uttered the words, "I love you," I still questioned it because it was happening extremely fast.

It was funny, because after Jason left, Jade couldn't get enough of what happened between us and needed every single detail.

Of course I took her advice and substituted Jason's name with the name Henry and Jade shrieked and clapped and yelled because as she said, "It was about damn time we got together."

I think she was more excited than I was that Jason and I had gotten together because in her own words, "Finally you two sealed the *fucking* deal. Pun definitely intended."

While I was happy to tell her about everything that happened between Jason and me, I wanted to question her on what happened with the two of them and why they ignored everybody the last month or so of school. I also wanted to ask her why she never told me about what happened when she and Jason were children, but I wasn't going to hold a grudge over it. I was just sad that she didn't open up to me about it, but I knew down the line she would open up to somebody about it and I couldn't wait for that moment to finally happen.

Jade deserved everything that Jason and I were starting to have and I just wanted to see her happy in the end. I knew that her finding a new guy to bring home every weekend was a way of rebelling and not getting hurt, but I often wondered who could tame Jade's wild side and get her to settle down. When it came down to it, I just wanted my friend to find happiness like I've found with her brother.

***

Tonight everyone was going to a local restaurant in downtown Baltimore to celebrate Sarah and Gabe getting married the next day. It was also the night that Jason and I were going to announce or show our friends that we had finally become a couple and I couldn't wait. I also couldn't wait to get back to our hotel room because Jason and I made plans to have wild, crazy sex all night long and I was already wet just thinking about it. I also had the vision of Jason looking down on me with a look of pure sex on his face while he said, "Yeah, we fucking do," when I said, "Well, I guess we have that settled then."

After pulling into the restaurant, Jade, Jason, and I all walked in. At first I was kind of nervous with everybody's reactions towards Jason and me dating now, but Jason eased my mind when he gently took my hand in his and intertwined our fingers together.

The hostess escorted us to a private room in the back and Jade walked in, yelling, "Party can start now, bitches!"

However Jason held me back and pushed me up against the wall, and before I could think, his mouth was on mine and our tongues was connecting. I must have made a sound because Jason chuckled and pulled away from me quickly. I wanted to protest but he just smiled and said, "Ready?"

I took a deep breath and said, "Yeah, I am." Not only was I answering Jason's question about walking into the private dinner room but I was also answering him for the secrets he was going to tell me eventually. I knew that nothing could keep us apart when we had to work so hard to get together in the first place. They were just bumps along the long and winding road now.

Putting an arm over my shoulder, we walked in and the room went from chatter and banter to complete silence in a matter of seconds. Everybody's eyes were on both Jason and I and they all had the same look of confusion, which quickly turned into excitement for the both of us.

Both Jason and I turned to look at one another at the same time and then I heard Sarah yell, "Well, kiss her already!"

Without taking his eyes off of me, he said, "With pleasure," and I knew there was a double meaning for later tonight.

He instantly picked me up by the hips and I wrapped my arms and legs around him just on instinct. I tried to lean in to kiss him but he had a hand on my lower back, holding me up, and the other was in my hair. He was holding onto my hair, controlling when he was going to kiss me and I started to laugh because we would get closer and closer but then he would pull back and I could hear groans coming from everybody. I thought they were going to explode but then Jason crushed his mouth to mine and swiped his tongue along my lower lip.

By the end of our *kiss* I was dizzy and unbelievably wet but before Jason put me down, he situated me so I could feel just how hard he was for me and I giggled.

Before setting me down on my feet he said, "That's how you make me feel, Ash, and I can't wait to make you come and scream my name later from just how hard I'll be fucking you."

To be honest, I just wanted to leave the dinner and go back to the hotel so we could get to this fucking sooner, but Jason must have read my mind because he whispered in my ear, "All in good time, Ash," and then kissed me on the cheek.

The dinner was amazing because it was a room filled with love and adoration for one another. Sarah and Gabe were getting married, Ryder and Isabelle were engaged, Jason and I were dating, and Jade was majorly hitting on our waiter. Derrick and Patrick were also there but because I hadn't told Jason my secret, they had to keep quiet about their relationship so they would give each other stolen glances and light brushes of fingertips underneath the table.

The speeches people gave were my favorite part because they were filled with love and laughter, especially Ryder's to both Sarah and Gabe:

"Sarah, you and I have been friends for as long as I can remember. We have grown up together and we have been through a lot. Love. Loss. Laughter. While I am humbled to be able to walk you down the aisle tomorrow, I can tell you that while your dad may not be there physically, I have no doubt he will be there spiritually along with the rest of us in this room, with tears in our eyes and smiles on our faces."

Winking at Sarah, Ryder turned his attention to Gabe. "To you, Gabe, you are my best friend and I was thrilled the day you walked up to Sarah and asked for her to cheer you on. I knew that you guys would last forever and I can tell you that if Sarah's dad were here, he would be saying those words to you as well. Finally, to the both of you: May your life together be filled with lots of love and zero regrets. Cheers, everybody!"

The looks on Sarah and Gabe's faces were priceless. You could tell that the friendships that Sarah and Ryder, as well as Gabe and Ryder shared were extremely special.

As soon as dinner was over I thought Jason would drag me out of the restaurant but he wrapped my hand in his and smiled down at me and said, "I love you, Ashlynn."

I'm not sure if the tears in my eyes were still from the speeches but when I closed my eyes, a tear fell down my face. When I opened my eyes, I saw Jason looking at me and the look wasn't of desire and passion but one of sincerity and almost like he was seeing me for the first time. I couldn't take it any longer and needed his lips on mine, so I wrapped my arms around his neck and stood on my tiptoes.

Before I said, "I love you, too," I kissed him and showed him just much I did love him.

The car ride back to the hotel was filled with complete silence, sexual silence. It was mainly silent because Jade said she would get a ride home later after she rode our waiter for the evening. Once we let ourselves into the room, Jason and I were on one another. I was ripping his shirt off him and he was pulling my dress up and over my head. With clothes falling to the floor, all I had on were my wedges, bra, and thong.

I started to step towards Jason, but while unbuckling the belt on his pants, he said, "Are you wet, Ash?"

I nodded because I could feel the wetness on my upper thighs, so I nodded my head.

Jason shook his head and said, "Are you wet, Ash?"

Not taking my eyes off his I said, "Yes, Jason, I'm wet."

He shook his head again and said, "How do you know you're wet?"

Again not taking my eyes away from him, I placed my hand in my panties and started making circles around my clit and said, "I can feel how wet I am."

I saw Jason's Adam's apple move up and down and while he took his pants off, he said, "Touch yourself, baby."

I thought doing this would be a little weird, but when Jason stood up, he started stroking himself and my mouth fell open. I never realized how sexual and hot it would be watching a guy stroke himself looking at you. I saw some pre-cum gather at the tip of his cock and I knew he wouldn't last long, which was totally fine with me because I knew with maybe a stroke or two, I would fall over the edge.

Releasing his grip on his cock, in a husky voice Jason said, "I want you to bend over the bed and move your legs apart."

I couldn't do something as simple as nod my head so I took my hand out of my panties and walked over to the bed but heard Jason say from behind me, "Keep touching yourself, Ash."

Reluctantly I placed my hand in my thong and rubbed slow circles again. I just couldn't take it any longer and needed Jason to be inside of me.

Bending over the bed, I heard Jason's footsteps coming up from behind me and my heart was beating so fast. I couldn't wait for him to be inside of me. He stopped right behind me and I could feel his hard cock up against my ass. He gave my ass a little slap and then said, "Spread your legs wider Ash, and lift your hips."

I did so willingly and before I knew it, Jason was ripping my thong from me and slamming right into me.

He moved all the way out and said, "Does that feel good, Ash?"

I just moaned my answer and heard Jason chuckle behind me and then he said, "What about this?" He pushed all the way inside of me and had this steady rhythm going where he swayed his hips. The first was amazing but the second was …

Fucking alarming,
Fucking breathing,
Motherfucking astounding!

I couldn't even warn him before I was coming and Jason thrust into me over and over again and rode my orgasm out. Somewhere along the way he had unclasped my bra and started pulling and rolling my nipples in his hands. My legs started to shake from just how powerful the orgasm was and Jason instantly wrapped an arm around my middle to hold me up. When I was able to gather myself, I pushed back against him and met him thrust for thrust.

Between grunts, Jason said, "Ash, I'm gonna fucking come," and I felt an orgasm quickly building.

There was something about Jason telling me he was going to come inside me that was overwhelming. I pushed back against him two more times and when I screamed, "Jason!" he roared, "Ashlynn!"

Catching our breath, we both fell onto the bed on our backs, looking up at the ceiling. I was about to turn over and look at Jason when the telephone rang.

The phone was right next to Jason, and without taking his eyes off the ceiling he grabbed the phone and breathlessly said, "Hello?"

I wondered who was calling us but then I heard Jason say, "I apologize. We'll keep it down," and then he hung up.

I already knew what it was and just started laughing when Jason turned on his side and said, "The manager called and said they were getting noise complaints about this room."

Shaking his head he said, "Fuck, Ashlynn, what are you doing to me?"

I slowly sat up and unclasped the wedges I was still wearing and dropped them onto the floor. I was thinking about just lying back down on the bed but decided to seductively turn around, and with a twinkle in my eye, I reached a hand out to touch Jason's cock. I knew he wasn't prepared because his eyes were still closed and I heard him take a deep breath in. I placed a leg on either side of him and slowly moved my hand up and down him, waiting for him to get hard in my hand.

I tortured him just like he'd tortured me only minutes ago. Jason started playing with my nipples, which only made me more aroused than I already was. He started thrusting into my hand and I let out a little giggle.

He looked up at me and said, "Something funny?"

I just cocked my head to the side and said, "Payback's a bitch, don't you think?"

His eyes got wide and said, "You little sneak."

As soon as those words left his mouth I leaned and whispered against his ear, "Let's really give 'em something to complain about, Jason," and lifting my hips, I slammed right down onto him.

He made this groaning, guttural sound and yelled, "Fuck!" at the top of his lungs. Placing my hands on the headboard, I moved up and down him quickly.

I never took my eyes off Jason the whole time I bounced up and down on him. I was moving up and down so fast that the bed began to creak and the headboard was slamming against the wall. Four strokes in and I could feel I was going to burst.

Gasping for air, I wailed, "I'm coming, Jason!" and he started moving his hips up and down and then came inside me and growled, "I love you, Ashlynn!"

I fell onto his sweaty chest while Jason rubbed up and down my back, soothing me. My eyes were beginning to close when the phone rang again and this time I picked it up.

"Hello?"

"Um, yes, this is management aga—"

I just cut them off and said, "I know. I'm sorry about the noise complaints. We're done now," and hung up.

Jason's chest was vibrating from laughing so hard and he said, "Really?" I couldn't do anything but laugh at us receiving noise complaints because of our phenomenal sex.

After catching my breath, I slid off him and laid down on my side, looking at how beautiful he was. Jason sat up in bed and pulled the covers over us and laid down on his side staring at me. No words needed to be said in that moment, because with just a look we could tell one another that we both loved each other.

I only closed my eyes for a minute but next thing I knew my alarm was going off the following morning.

Rolling over in bed, I saw Jason staring back at me and I giggled. He nudged me onto my back and said, "How are you feeling today?" I started to move around and realized I was actually pretty sore from last night. He must have seen from the way I moved my body because he said, "I'm sorry; I just kind of lost control last night with you."

I just laughed and said, "Jason, I'm not made of glass. You're not going to break me. Yes, I'm sore but I enjoyed last night, if you couldn't tell. Plus every time I move my body today, images of last night will be coming across in my mind and I'll have a smile plastered to my face because of it."

With that explanation, Jason kissed me on the lips and then carried me into the bathroom where he washed me as I sat on the built in seat. I told him it wasn't necessary but he just shook it off and said he wanted to take care of me.

Being a girl, I couldn't help but think because we were going to a wedding today and the way he looked at me and said, "I want to take care of you, Ashlynn," had me thinking that not only did he want to take care of me in the showe,r but maybe in life as well. But while I wanted to believe him, I knew that he wasn't telling me everything and I wanted to know why.

He must have sensed the hesitation on my face because he said, "I'll tell you later, Ashlynn, but right now I want to enjoy our time together."

His words scared me and I didn't know what to think. I hated that this had to happen on a day when our friends were getting married.

While Sarah and Gabe were standing before God and their friends and family announcing their love for one another, my heart was sinking because I was petrified at what Jason would have to tell me. I had a feeling it would be something to do with his dad or mom. Maybe even the both of them.

I just wasn't sure and I was scared to death because I didn't want what happened last time when we were in Florida to happen this time after everything that had happened between us. I didn't want him to close off from me and ignore me because so much had changed between the two of us.

Chapter 11

Jason

Everything was going exceptionally between Ashlynn and me. I felt like this could be the real deal, which is why I asked her dad for his permission for me to marry her. I knew we wouldn't get married anytime soon, but I knew with all of my heart someday I was going to make her mine. While talking to my dad did some good, I was nowhere near ready for thinking about having children, and I wasn't sure I ever would be. I just hoped that Ashlynn would be okay with that when we did get married someday, because I knew that when I looked into my future without a shadow of a doubt Ashlynn was in mine forever.

While I knew I made my own choices in life on what I wanted and who I wanted, there was still a small part of me that questioned whether or not I would become just like my dad later in life. Like our time in Florida, everything was perfect up until the day of Sarah and Gabe's wedding. I could see it in Ashlynn's eyes that she wanted to know just why exactly I had ignored her for a while after Spring Break ended but I didn't want it to be the day of the wedding, so I said, "I'll tell you later, Ashlynn, but right now I want to enjoy our time together."

I thought saying that would put her mind at ease, but she flinched back from me and mentally guarded herself as well. I could see it in her eyes and in her demeanor the entire wedding. While she was laughing and crying, I could tell that her mind was somewhere else, and by somewhere else I mean thinking about what I was going to tell her. It wasn't a huge secret, it was just something I had to deal with before I could start a real relationship with Ashlynn. I didn't want to bring in extra baggage. That's the important part and really what she needed to understand.

During the reception, Jade walked up to me and asked, "All right, spill, Jason. What's up with you and Ashlynn?"

I just shrugged my shoulders and said, "Not now, Jade. I'm really not in the mood to talk at the moment."

It really made her concerned and she pulled me into a corner., "Seriously, what's going on, Jason? You're kind of scaring me."

Taking a long gulp of my beer, I said, "I still haven't explained everything that happened with Dad to Ashlynn yet. I mean, I told her about our childhood and everything, but not about the phone call and what happened when we met up with him at the end of the school year."

Jade's mouth dropped open at my confession and she was speechless, probably for the first time in her life. Tilting her head to the side in a low voice, she said, "You told her about what happened to you?"

Shaking my head, I said, "Correction, Jade, I told her about what happened to both of us." She flinched and I thought she was going to cry, so I pulled her into my arms. She wrapped her arms around my middle and then I felt wetness on my shirt and knew my sister was crying.

I put her at arm's length and asked, "Why are you crying, Jade?"

My question just made her cry even more, so I pulled her back to me and held onto her so she could calm down and explain to me what was going on. Getting herself under control, she said, "I'm sorry, Jason." I didn't understand where her apology was coming from so I questioned her on it.

Shrugging her shoulders, she said, "I'm crying for what happened to you. I'm crying because I didn't do a damn thing to help you when we were little. I'm crying because Ashlynn is my best friend and I never told her. I was just so ashamed of what went on in our household. I was also ashamed that I never did anything to help you and sometimes I feel like our mom. She knew what was going on and she never did anything. Our father beat you and I just stood there and watched, just like her."

Her lip started to quiver and before I knew it she was crying again.

I quickly pulled her against me and started murmuring reassurance into her ear. "Jade, you're nothing like Mom, do you hear me? None of what happened to us is your fault. We were both kids and I don't blame you for, in your own words, 'not doing anything.' I love you, Jade, and I would do anything for you, I hope you know that. I'm positive with every bone in my body that Ashlynn doesn't hate you. She might be hurt but I know she could never hate you for not telling her what happened to us. You hear me, li'l sis?"

My question made her giggle and she nodded her head up and down against my chest. She then squeezed me to her. "Only by four minutes, but I love you, big brother."

Giving Jade one last hug, I noticed out of the corner of my eye that Ashlynn was looking at us and I knew that I had to tell her as soon as possible what all happened to Jade and I a month and a half ago.

Later that night when we got back to the hotel from the reception, we both got undressed and snuggled up in bed. We were both lying on our sides and her back was to my front. My arm was draped over her middle and I knew she could feel my heart beating extremely fast. I was just about to say her name when I heard these little purring sounds and knew that my Ashlynn was asleep. Kissing the back of her head, I said, "Goodnight, babe," and drifted off to sleep in the comfort of holding Ashlynn to me.

Upon checking out the next morning, we made the drive back to our apartments. I dropped Jade off at the apartment, but when Ashlynn was getting ready to get out, I placed a hand over hers.

She looked at me with sadness in her eyes and I asked, "Could you come over to my apartment for a little while? I just wanted to talk to you about everything."

I wanted to take the look in her eyes away so badly because she looked like she was just going to burst into tears any second, but she put on a brave face and nodded her head. As soon as I saw Jade walk into their apartment, I drove off to mine. The car ride was silent and it gave me time to collect my bearings to inform Ashlynn on what all exactly happened.

Parking the car, I left my bags in the trunk and Ashlynn and I walked into my apartment. I was relieved that Neil wasn't there because I wanted to do this in private. Ashlynn sat down on the sofa and I went to the fridge to get a bottle of water.

I looked over in Ash's direction and asked, "Ashlynn, do you want a drink?"

In this timid voice she said, "No, Jason."

Closing the fridge, I walked over to the sofa and sat down next to her. Taking a deep breath, I explained everything. "That last night in Florida, I received a call from my dad. He asked if we could talk, and as much as I didn't want to, I figured I might as well just listen to what he had to say. From what I told you before about mine and Jade's childhood, you know it was pretty difficult having to hear his voice and I was emotionally drained after that short conversation. Truthfully, I just didn't know how to tell you. I wanted to get the future conversation over with before you and I ever started anything because you are extremely important to me, Ashlynn Miller.

"Anyway, when we got back to school, I called him and he informed me that he was dying of cancer. I didn't know what to say, so I just listened to him. He apologized for everything that he did. He explained how I was nothing like him. He said that I was so much more. He said I was such a better person than him."

I was still explaining when I felt Ashlynn place her hand on top of mine for comfort and I looked over at her and saw her tears falling. I put my other hand to her cheek and used my thumb to wipe away the tears and she gave me a small smile.

Clearing my throat, I continued.

"While it was difficult to hear that, I knew I had to tell Jade. When I did, she pretty much lost it and then informed me that she wanted to see him. She needed to talk to him and come to her own form of closure, so that's what she did. I went with her back to our hometown and was there for her when she talked to our father. I didn't think seeing him would be all that hard on me, but I was wrong. He just looked so fragile and weak and now his outer appearance matched his inner. He apologized profusely to the both of us and asked if we could find it in our hearts to forgive him. He also wanted to be a part of our lives now and be given an attempt to make up for what he did to our childhoods."

I took a break to let everything seep in with Ashlynn.

A few minutes later she cleared her throat and asked, "What do you want to do, Jason?"

I looked over at her and asked, "What do you mean?"

Holding onto my hand, she asked, "Do you want to try and build or repair a relationship with your dad?"

Shaking my head, I gave her my honest answer. "I don't know."

Taking a sip of my bottle of water, Ashlynn said, "I'll be here for you no matter what you choose, Jason."

The only thing I was one hundred percent positive about was that I would always choose Ashlynn and I told her so.

I got up from the sofa and picked her up in my arms. "I'll always choose you, Ash. No matter what," and then carried her back to my room and closed the door.

That night I showed her just how much I loved her and how deeply I felt about her. I took my time with her, tasting every single bit of her body and touching every part of her I could get my hands on. I had her whimpering and moaning and screaming my name. I had her writhing and coming undone beneath me. There were even a few tears shed, and if I had any doubt before telling Ashlynn, I knew now that she would be mine forever.

A few hours later we both lay on our sides facing one another and talked into the early morning. Our conversation started with favorite movies, music, and books. We talked about what we both wanted to do over the summer. I got a laugh out of her when I just said, "You."

Her laugh just did something to me. I loved that I could get that smile on her face and make her eyes twinkle and sparkle and glisten. Our talk then got more serious when she asked about what I wanted to do when it came to starting a relationship with my dad.

Looking deep into her eyes, I said, "I don't know, Ashlynn."

I didn't even realize I was crying until she placed a hand to my face and wiped the tears away. She leaned into me and slowly kissed my tears away, and after making love again, Ashlynn nuzzled up to me, resting her head on my chest.

Drawing lazy circles on my stomach with her fingers, she whispered, "I lost my mom when I was younger and I never got to say goodbye. She was such an amazing person and I just wish that my dad and I were given the chance to say goodbye to her or say I love you one last time, but we didn't get that option."

Lifting her head to look at me, she said, "But you and Jade do. I'm not saying that you have to say, 'I love you,' but I do think that you haven't found your closure yet with what happened when you were younger. I'm not condoning what he did, but I think that sometimes it takes something life-threatening like cancer to realize what's important in life or show you how badly you messed up in yours."

Biting her lip, she said, "I think your dad had to find that out the hard way. Ultimately, the choice is yours on what you decide to do, but I just wanted to give you my thoughts on it."

Getting up on my elbows, I wrapped a hand around the back of Ashlynn's neck and whispered against her lips, "I love you, Ashlynn," and before kissing me, she said, "I love you, Jason."

We fell asleep tangled up in one another's arms, but a few hours later I was woken up by Ashlynn jumping up out of bed and running into the bathroom. I quickly put on some boxers in case Neil was home and ran in to see Ashlynn's head was in the toilet. She was throwing up. I knelt down next to her and rubbed her back while she threw up everything and then dry heaved.

Once she was finished emptying everything in her stomach, I picked her up and carried her back to my room and laid her down in my bed. I then walked back to the bathroom and flushed the toilet and got a washcloth and ran it under some cold water. As soon as I was walking back to the room to place it on Ashlynn's head, she was running towards the bathroom again. This time she closed the door and locked it so I couldn't get in.

I sat outside and waited for her and a few minutes later she came out and said, "Jason, can you take me home?"

My heart stopped because I didn't understand why she wanted me to take her back to her apartment but reluctantly I said, "Yeah, I'll just get some shorts on and take you."

While she waited for me to get dressed, she waved her hands back and forth and said, "It's just the flu and I don't want you to get sick."

She walked up behind me and turned me around. Wrapping her arms around my neck, she looked at me, smiled, and said, "So please stop worrying," and placed a kiss on my cheek.

Before I dropped her off at the apartment, I stopped at the grocery store and picked up some ginger ale, chicken soup, and a new movie that came out. When I got back in the car, she laughed at me and said, "I love you, Jason Williams."

When I parked the car, I carried Ashlynn to her apartment. There were people staring but I didn't care. I just looked at them and said, "The girl I love is sick, so give me a break." I knew Ashlynn's face was bright red but she hid her face in my neck.

Getting her comfortable in her bed, I went back down to the car and carried up her bag from the weekend and the bag filled with groceries. I quickly made her chicken soup and poured a glass of ginger ale and began to walk back to her room. But by the time I got there, she was fast asleep.

I decided to just pour the soup into a container and drink the ginger ale. I was just cleaning up the dishes when Jade walked in and her jaw dropped at the sight.

Plopping down at the breakfast bar, she giggled and said, "You're looking quite domestic today." Still washing the pot, I looked up at her and said, "Ash isn't feeling good. I made her some chicken noodle soup but she fell asleep already. I'm going to head out, but could you just let me know how she's doing?"

Jade just nodded her head up and down and smiled.

I dropped the washrag and looked at her. "What exactly are you smiling about, Jade?"

She just shrugged her shoulders and so nonchalantly said, "I'm just really happy for you guys. I'm happy you finally realized what was there right in front of you this entire time. You deserve some happiness."

Wiping my hands on a towel, I walked over to her and pulled her into my arms. She wrapped her arms around me, and talking into her hair, I said, "You deserve to be happy, too."

Pulling back from me, she said, "Jason, that would just be a big mistake right now. You know, with everything that's going on with Dad? I just don't need that right now."

Kissing her on the forehead, I said, "All right, well, I'll talk to you soon."

"Yeah, Jason, I'll let you know how she's doing in a little bit."

With my hand on the front door, I turned to Jade and said, "Take care of my girl, sis," and left.

The rest of the day I tried to stay busy by doing laundry, cleaning my room, and the kitchen. Neil thought I was smoking some sort of crack or something because I was on a cleaning spree. I quickly warned him not to get used to it and told him how Ashlynn wasn't feeling good and it just wasn't sitting right with me.

Neil just laughed and slapped me on the back. "You need to relax, bro. Come on, there's a game on tonight, so let's go down to the bar, have some cold beers and hot wings, and get your mind off your girl."

Emily McKee

I was reluctant but decided to get out of the house. Halfway through the game, Jade texted me:

Jade – Ash is fine, she just has a stomach bug.

I was relieved that she was feeling better but I just wished that it was Ash who was texting me but she needed her rest. Once the game was over, Neil and I headed back to the apartment and crashed for the night. Just before I fell asleep, I texted Ash:

Jason – I hope you're feeling better soon baby. I love you and good night.

I waited a little while but when I didn't get a text back, I fell asleep with a smile on my face, dreaming of my past, present, and what the future holds for me and Ashlynn.

Chapter 12

Ashlynn

I couldn't believe how sick I was. I felt bad for asking Jason to take me home but I didn't want him to catch what I had and have to lie in bed along with me. *Although? No, no.*

As soon as Jason tucked me into bed, I passed out. I don't even think my head was on the pillow for two seconds before I was fast asleep. Throwing up just took it out of me and I felt really weak. I didn't wake up till later in the afternoon and after taking a long hot shower, I changed and walked out into the living room.

Jason was so sweet and decided to pick me up a movie while he was at the grocery store picking up soup and ginger ale. I didn't know what movie it was until I walked out into the living room and saw Jade opening the DVD case to *The Vow* with Rachel McAdams and Channing Tatum. Jade looked up at me and we both just started laughing hysterically at the memory this movie held for us.

Since Jade and I were both single on Valentine's Day, we'd decided to go see that movie because it looked really good. Plus Channing Tatum was in it and you can't beat that!

On our way to the movie theatre, Jade texted Jason and asked what he was doing that night. When he texted back that he wasn't doing anything, both Jade and I turned to each other with mischief all over our faces and decided to kidnap him and drag him along with us to the movies because we didn't want him to be alone on Valentine's Day. At first he didn't want to come with us, but we promised to get him a huge bucket of popcorn and any kind of candy his little heart desired.

The second we mentioned food, Jason was on board, but little did he know he would have to sit through a two hour movie with a bunch of single girls in the theatre. For the most part, Jason was a good sport but halfway through we could tell he was bored out of his mind. He kept checking his phone and I think at one point he even fell asleep, but as soon as it ended, everybody started clapping and cheering because Rachel McAdams and Channing Tatum finally got back together.

There were all of these screaming girls cheering and then out of nowhere you heard Jason screaming, "Fucking finally!" If the movie theatre wasn't loud with laughter and cheers before, it was then.

Once Jade and I wiped the tears falling from our faces and controlled our laughter, I plopped down onto the sofa and snuggled under a blanket while Jade put the DVD into the player.

She started to walk over to the couch but went to the kitchen instead. I heard her cracking open a can while she said, "Jason got you ginger ale and some soup. Are you hungry?"

As soon as she asked me, my stomach made the loudest growling sound known to man. I guess Jade could hear it because she said, "I guess so."

Getting out from underneath the blanket, I went over and sat down at the breakfast bar. I started to take a sip of my ginger ale when Jade opened the container for the soup and before I knew it I had my hand to my mouth and I was running to the bathroom.

I barely made it to the toilet before I was throwing up. I hadn't eaten anything today because I slept it away, so it was just stomach acid and then a bunch of dry heaving. By the time my stomach settled, I looked over and saw Jade was staring at me with a weird look on her face.

Standing, I walked over to the sink and grabbed my toothbrush. Squeezing out toothpaste onto the brush I said, "All right, Jade, what's with the face?"

Wetting the brush, I put it into my mouth and began to brush away the disgusting taste in my mouth while I waited for Jade to spill. I looked over at her with a confused look on my face and she was staring at my stomach with wide eyes and an open mouth. I didn't understand what she was acting so weird about so I just went back to brushing my teeth. I could see her in the mirror still staring at my stomach and that's when it hit me.

The brush fell from my hand into the sink and looking at her through the mirror I screamed, "Holy fuckballs!"

I quickly spit out the excess toothpaste and ran into my room like a fucking lunatic and searched for my purse. The second I found my purse, I unzipped it and found my birth control packet. Sliding the pills out, I looked at the remaining tablets and my mouth dropped. I ran over to my nightstand table and unplugged my phone and searched the application I had downloaded, which was a period calendar.

With the phone in one hand and the birth control pills in the other, I looked up and saw Jade staring at me.

I let out some pathetic noise and then Jade said, "Okay, I know you and my brother had sex and I know you're a smart girl, Ash. So please, for the love of all that is good in this world, tell me that Jason wore a condom."

I made another pathetic noise and then Jade screamed, "Are you fucking psychotic?"

I was still stunned when Jade walked over to me and pushed me back so I was sitting on my bed. Taking the birth control packet and phone from my hands, she placed them on the nightstand.

Turning back to me, she sat down on the bed and said, "Spill right now!" I looked over at her and a tear fell down my face because of the realization I might have to face.

Taking a deep breath, I wiped the tears away and explained everything.

"The first time we had sex, Jason didn't have a condom and I told him I was on birth control. We were both just caught up in the moment and it happened. After that, um, we just didn't."

I was too embarrassed to look at Jade's face when I told her but when I looked up at her, the emotions just hit me. I mean I ugly cried. Tears were falling down my face, my chin was quivering, my face was scrunching together and I'm pretty sure boogers were running out of my nose.

I don't know when it happened, but next thing I knew I was cradled in Jade's arms while she tried to calm me down. Running her fingers through my hair, she said, "Ashlynn, we don't know if you're pregnant yet, so please calm down."

Calming down was the last thing on my mind. I immediately got out of the warmth I felt being embraced in Jade's arms and word spewed everything I had running through my mind.

Looking at her, I said, "But what if I am pregnant? Jason's already said that he doesn't want to have children. He doesn't want to mess up their lives the way your dad messed up both of yours. I feel like as soon as Jason and I are okay, something comes along and just messes it all up and I don't know what I'm going to do. What am I supposed to say to him? I mean, I told him I was on birth control and I was, but I might be pregnant. Oh my god, he's going to think I lied to hi—"

"You stop right there, Ashlynn Paisley Miller! Yes, you guys didn't use a condom the first time, but certainly Jason carried condoms in his wallet or his pocket or glued to his motherfucking hand the other times after that. This is not all your fault! Yes, Jason and I had a messed up childhood, but if you are pregnant, I know my brother will take care of that child. Ashlynn, he loves you, and if you can't see that yet, then you are seriously messed up."

Taking a few calming breaths, I said, "I know Jason loves me, but it just seems like we can't catch a break. As soon as we find happiness, it just all gets messed up again and I don't know what to do. I don't even know how to tell him."

Wrapping her arms around me, Jade kissed me on the cheek and said, "You take a nice long bath and I'll be back with the essentials. No matter what, Ashlynn, it's going to be okay."

Giving her a squeeze, I said, "Thanks, Jade, I love you."

Kissing me on the cheek, she said, "Well, I love your dumb ass, too," which got me to smile just a tiny bit. Releasing one another, I looked at her. She must have sensed me staring at her because after she got off the bed, she looked at me and asked, "What?"

Tilting my head to the side I asked, "How'd you come to the conclusion that you thought I was pregnant?"

Looking into my eyes, she said, "We don't know if you're pregnant yet, but when Mom was pregnant with Jason and I, she couldn't stand the smell and look of meat, especially chicken. It just really grossed her out and she's been a vegetarian ever since."

I must have had a worried look on my face because Jade walked over to me and tilting my chin up, she said, "It's going to be okay, Ashlynn. Everything will be okay. Now smile that beautiful smile you have going on and show your bestie all those pearly whites you've got going on there."

Giving her a halfass smile, she left my room and said, "I'll be back."

As soon as I heard the front door close, my heart dropped and I started crying. I just couldn't believe the mess I got myself in now and I didn't have the slightest clue how to get out of it. There was just something in me telling me that I already knew the answer, that I was pregnant. Getting up off the bed, I walked over to the nightstand table and turned my phone off. I just needed my own time to think about what I was going to do and how I was going to tell Jason.

I decided to take Jade's advice and take a warm bubble bath to just try and calm myself. After starting the bath and adding the bubbles, I went back into my room and got my Kindle because I definitely needed an escape from my life right now.

I needed to read about people who didn't get pregnant even though the girl was on birth control. I needed to read about fictional characters who could mess up beyond repair and somehow the author thought it was humanly possible to not have to face the consequences because right now I wished I was one of those characters.

Unfortunately, real life isn't like that. It's not a place where you can mess up and get away with it. Every day we gamble. We are given decisions and we make our choices. But it's because of those choices we are where we are and we can't blame anybody for that besides ourselves when we royally fuck up.

I turned on my Kindle and started up where I left off on the last book in the *Fifty Shades* trilogy and maybe five minutes into reading, Anastasia found out she was pregnant.

Like seriously? I just went off about how authors write and make it possible in the universe of fictional fucked-upness that a character can get out of any mess and what do you know? Fucking Anastasia Steele is pregnant while on birth control!

Throwing my Kindle on the floor, I pulled my legs up to my chest and cried because I didn't know what else to do. Not even reading could help me escape. As if I couldn't feel worse, the memory of Jason and I making love in the bathtub at the hotel drifted its way into my mind.

The way he held me so close to him and looked into my eyes whispering words like:

"I'll never leave you."

"I love you, Ash."

"Forever and always."

A little while later, I heard the front door open and close and then there was a knock on the bathroom door. "Ashlynn?"

Not taking my head out of the crook of my legs, I mumbled, "You can come on in, Jade."

With a twist of the knob she peeked in and said, "I've got some pregnancy tests, crackers, and some more ginger ale. So whenever you're ready."

I still hadn't moved my head. Again I mumbled, "I'll just be out in a minute."

I heard her put a bag on the floor and once the door was closed, I rinsed myself off and got out of the tub and wrapped myself up in a towel. Going back into my room, I dried off and put on some yoga pants and a t-shirt. Taking a deep breath, I walked back into the bathroom and closed the door behind me. Jade had left the bag of pregnancy tests in there. As if I didn't already know my fate.

Opening the box, I pulled out the stick and read the instructions. Following them, I set the stick on the side of the sink, washed my hands, and dragged my pregnant ass out into the living room where Jade was sitting quietly waiting for me.

I fell down next to her and held her hand while I waited for the answer I already knew the test was going to give me. We both sat there and stared at the blank television for the two longest minutes of our lives. Once the timer went off, we both got up off the couch and, never releasing the hold of our hands, walked back into the bathroom. Even though I knew the answer, my heart was still beating rapidly. Picking up the stick, I looked down and read the single hardest word out there for me at this moment.

Pregnant.

***

It had been two days since I found out I was going to be a mom and Jason was going to be a dad and I still didn't have the slightest clue on how I was going to tell him. I decided today was going to be the day that the truth was going to come out; that we were going to be parents in eight and a half months. I just needed two days to maybe come up with some kind of miracle way of telling him but of course no miracle had fallen into my pregnant lap.

Some may think it was childish of me to ignore his text messages but every time I read words like:

... I love you baby.
... can't wait to hold you in my arms baby.
... you okay baby?

my heart dropped, my stomach tightened and I threw up. Of course the throwing up was not only from nerves but morning sickness as well.

Getting my purse from my room, I started to open the front door when Jade said, "Give me the keys; I'll drive."

I turned and looked at her. "You're coming with me?"

Jade shrugged her shoulders and said, "Yeah, I'm coming with you. Did you think I was not going to?"

Shaking my head back and forth, I said, "I didn't expect you to. That's all."

She grabbed me in a big hug. Jade whispered, "Like I said before. I'm going to be here every step of the way; no matter what the outcome is, Ash."

Pulling back, I wiped the tears away from my face and said, "All right, let's do this."

The drive over to Jason's apartment was unbearable. Every foot we drove I wanted to beg Jade to just turn around and drive away. But we can't drive or hide away from our problems because the truth will come out. Or in my case, show the truth when my stomach grew because of the child growing inside.

It seemed like we got there faster than normal but Jade said, "Damn, I even drove slow."

Laughing at her comment, I got out of the car and made my way over to Jade. I was so grateful she came with me because I needed her support in this. Taking her hand in mine, we walked up to Jason's apartment and I slowly reached my hand up and knocked on the door.

Jason opened it and this huge smile came across his face and he was reaching out to me and lifting me up to his arms. Kissing me on the lips, he walked us back into his apartment and said, "I missed you, baby. You're looking a lot better. How are you feeling?"

Jade walked in behind us and closed the door and then met eye contact with me. She nodded her head in reassurance so I looked to Jason and said, "I'm feeling better."

I thought I sounded okay but Jason tilted his head and asked, "Are you sure?"

I couldn't lie to him again so I just nodded my head, hoping that was a good enough answer. Grabbing my hand, he pulled me into the living room and said, "Sit down. You want something to drink?"

Jade was walking over when I said, "Water, please."

Once Jason walked into the kitchen, Jade sat next to me and whispered, "It's going to be okay but you have to tell him."

At that moment, Jason walked out and handed me a bottle of water. "Tell me what?" Sitting down, he placed an arm over my shoulder and rubbed.

Turning towards him I smiled and said, "How much I missed you." He leaned in and kissed me on the lips.

The second his lips touched mine, Neil came walking in and said, "Hey, get a room for that stuff," and I instantly stiffened.

I saw Jason look at me and knew that he saw, but he looked over at Neil and said, "Oh, it was a little kiss on the lips, chill."

Neil laughed and waved his arms, saying, "Forget about it," but then he noticed Jade was in the room and turned towards her and said, "But I will not forget your beautiful face anytime soon, doll."

I didn't get to hear Jade's reply because Jason said, "Don't even think about it, dude. Big mistake." Neil just laughed and turned on the television, settling on some movie.

I was too busy trying to figure out how I was going to tell Jason that I kind of zoned out while everybody else watched the movie, but once it was over, Jason got up and pulled me along with him into his room. Neil had a witty comment but I didn't hear because of how loud my heart was pounding in my chest.

Once we reached his room, Jason closed the door behind him and said, "What's going on, Ash?"

Those four words were my undoing and I just cried. I felt Jason's arms wrap around me and I just cried even more. I wrapped my arms around his neck and buried my head into his chest while he settled his head on top of mine.

Rubbing his hands up and down my back, he whispered, "It's okay, Ash. It's okay."

I broke away from him and said, "No, it's not okay. This is just a huge mess and I don't know what to do. I don't know how to tell you."

Walking up to me, Jason looked into my eyes and said, "All right, Ash, what's the matter? You're really scaring me here."

I lowered my head and took a deep breath. Lifting my head to look into Jason's eyes, I whispered, "I'm pregnant."

Chapter 13

Jason

I was starting to get really nervous because Ashlynn wasn't texting me back and it had been two days since I dropped her off at her apartment. Jade would text me every once in a while, telling me that Ashlynn was getting better, but something just wasn't sitting right with me. I needed to hear her voice. I was just getting ready to leave my apartment to surprise Ash when there was a knock at my door.

Opening the door, I saw Ashlynn and Jade standing there and I couldn't believe it. I was so relieved to see Ash that I just needed to kiss her. So I picked her up in my arms and walked us back into the apartment, kissing her. I wanted to take her back to my room and have my way with her, but there was something about the way she was acting that made me a little nervous. While I was happy to see my sister, I just wanted some alone time with Ash.

I was just getting ready to sit down next to Ash when I heard Jade whisper, "It's going to be okay but you have to tell him."

My heart plummeted so I said, "Tell me what?"

Handing her the bottle of water and sitting down, I could tell from her demeanor that something was way off. She was as stiff as a board and I could see her gnawing on her lower lip.

Turning to me, she smiled and said, "How much I missed you." I knew she wasn't lying about missing me but I could tell something just wasn't right and I needed to get to the bottom of it.

I was just about to ask her to come back to my room with me when Neil walked out, so we started to watch a movie. Throughout the movie, I kept peeking over at Ashlynn and she was either picking her nails or biting on her lower lip, which just made me scatter-brained until I couldn't take it anymore. The movie barely finished before I was pulling her up from the couch and dragging her back to my room. My brain had gotten the worst of me and I started thinking that maybe she wanted to break up with me or she cheated on me or something awful.

I could hear her breathing heavily behind me and once we got in my room, I closed the door and turned to her. "What's going on, Ash?" I had to know what the fuck was going on.

I didn't think I said it too rudely, but she just broke down in tears. She began to hiccup and I just ran over to her and hugged her.

I tried to calm her down "It's okay, Ash. It's okay," I reassured her, but she pushed me away from her.

"No, it's not okay. This is just a huge mess and I don't know what to do. I don't know how to tell you."

I knew she was going to break up with me and I didn't think I could take it anymore. I just wanted her to come clean about it. As much as it would completely suck, I had to hear her say it. Her back was against my bedroom wall so I walked over and caged her in. "All right, Ash, what's the matter? You're really scaring me."

She lowered head and let out a breath and then whispered, "I'm pregnant."

My jaw dropped open and I looked at her. I didn't know what else to do. Her face started to scrunch up and she started shifting her weight from foot to foot. Blinking a few times, I said, "I'm sorry, but what did you just say, Ash?"

A little bit louder she said, "I'm pregnant, Jason."

I dropped my arms to my side and just started walking backwards toward the bed. I needed to sit down as soon as possible or I thought I might pass out. As soon as I sat down, I put my head in my hands and said, "I can't."

I mean what the fuck was I supposed to do? I had just come to the conclusion that it was going to be okay to date Ashlynn and I wouldn't mess it up, but kids? I sure as hell wasn't ready for that. And as much as my dad said I wouldn't be like him, there was still that small amount of me that questioned whether I would treat my own kids like that some day. I knew I couldn't fast forward time and look into the future, so I just figured I would cut the family ties and not risk it. I couldn't live with myself if I ever treated my own kids the way my dad treated Jade and I growing up.

Before I knew it, I was lifting my head towards Ash's direction but she wasn't there. I quickly got up from the bed and ran out into the living room, but the only person out there was Neil, who was sitting at the breakfast bar with the same look I had on my face.

Jaw dropped and eyes wide open.

Running over to him I yelled, "Where are they?"

Neil blinked and looked at me. "They left, dude. Ashlynn was in tears and Jade looked pissed beyond belief."

I walked over and fell on the couch, leaning my head back. I didn't know what the fuck I was supposed to do. This was all just happening so damn fast. I heard Neil walk over to the fridge and grab two bottles of beer. Walking over to me, he handed me one and then took a sip of his own. I lifted the bottle to my lips and chugged the whole thing down. After setting the bottle down on the end table, I leaned back and closed my eyes.

There was no question that I loved Ashlynn Miller but I was frightened that I would become just like my dad. That guy was a selfish prick and thought he walked on water, but right now I was trying to do the right thing. I thought I was being selfless by letting Ash leave because I could have grabbed my keys and sped over there. I could have dropped to my knees and begged for forgiveness and we could have lived happily ever after, but this was reality. In that moment I thought I was doing the right thing by staying away.

Letting out a breath, I opened my eyes and saw Neil's demeanor hadn't changed. His mouth and eyes were still both wide open, so I asked, "What the fuck is that face for?"

Blinking, he looked at me and said, "So off topic, but fuck, your sister is hot when she gets pissed."

Shaking my head back and forth, I said, "Like I said before, Neil, that's a big mistake. You really don't want to mess with me right now."

Taking a sip of his beer, he got up and said, "You asked." He walked back to his bedroom and just as his door closed, the front door opened.

I turned around just in time to see Jade storming towards me. I quickly got up and said, "What the fuck are you doing here?" I probably shouldn't have said that because she walked right up to me and slapped me hard across the face. I was stunned that Jade had slapped me across the face. Lifting my hand to my face, I said, "What the fuck was that for?"

Putting her hands on her hips, she said, "I was trying to slap the stupid out of that fucking head of yours. What the hell is your problem? I thought you loved Ashlynn and you didn't say anything to her. I thought you were going to be happy about this. Ashlynn is carrying your child. You're going to be a dad. Yes, it's a lot to take in and you guys are young, but you love one another."

Sitting down, I said, "Jade, that's why I can't do this."

Walking back and forth in front of me, she yelled, "What the fuck does that mean? And don't you dare give me some bullshit excuse, Jason Williams."

Oh fuck. Jade was seriously pissed because she never said my middle name.

Looking up at her, I just started crying. Jade knelt and wrapped her arms around me and said, "What's going on, Jason? I'm your sister, for fuck's sake. Please tell me what's going on in that head of yours."

Letting go of me, she got up off the floor and sat down next to me on the couch. She took hold of my hand and started rubbing her thumb back and forth along the top, trying to calm me. I looked over at Jade and she looked scared out of her mind.

"I can't be like dad, Jade. I can't and won't do that to my children. If our childhood didn't wound us and leave scars to remind us every damn day that we didn't have a normal childhood, whatever the fuck that is, I wouldn't be sitting here with you holding my hand. I would be ecstatic and twirling Ash around because she's carrying my child and we're going to have a baby together. It has nothing to do with being scared because I'm only twenty-one. I'm scared because I don't want to hurt my child the way Dad hurt us."

Jade moved all the way over and wrapped her arms around me while I broke down again. I held on to my sister like she was the only thing keeping me here. She was the only one who could possibly understand why I was doing what I did and be okay with my decision.

Finally calming myself, I let go of Jade and leaned back against the couch.

She was still sitting in the same position as before and, without taking her eyes off me, she said, "Jason, you have told me that I am nothing like Mom and I never will be. I have been carrying this guilt around with me for so long. So please tell me why it's different for me but not for you?"

Closing my eyes, I said, "Because you're a good person, Jade."

She took my hand in hers. "Dammit, open your eyes, Jason."

Opening my eyes, I looked over at Jade and she had tears welling up in hers. "How could you possibly think you aren't a good person? You took all of the beatings when we were little because you wouldn't let him come near me. I just watched and did nothing. You love your unborn child so much that you would rather be away from him or her for the rest of your life than become just like Dad. You are the most selfless, best person I know and that is why I can tell you that right now you are making a mess of this situation."

I really needed to hear Jade tell me that. Growing up, I had always told Jade that she was nothing like Mom, so why then would I think I would end up like Dad? In the end, we were two people who had our own minds and could make our own decisions. We didn't need the influence of both our fucked up parents to come to those conclusions on our own.

Wrapping my sister in my arms, I kissed her on the top of the head and got up from the couch.

Jade jumped up and said, "Where are you going, Jason?"

I grabbed my keys off the breakfast bar and said, "I'm going to go see my girl and my baby."

With a big smile across her face and tears in her eyes, Jade said, "Go get the both of them, Jason, and never let go."

My hand was on the door handle but I ran back over to Jade and hugged her again. Leaning away from her, I said, "Thanks, Jade, I don't know where I would be without you. I love you so much."

Smiling up at me, she said, "I love you too, Jason, now go."

Winking at her, I ran out of the front door, hopped in the car, and sped towards my future.

I tried to drive as fast as I could without getting pulled over by the cops but it still took the longest six minutes of my life. Doing a half ass parking job, I jumped out of the car, bolted up the stairs and knocked and knocked and knocked until the front door opened to Ash and Jade's apartment.

Ashlynn opened the door and the view took my breath away. Even though her eyes were swollen from crying, her nose was red, and her face was scrunched up, I still had a huge smile on my face. Looking away from her face, I looked down at her stomach and couldn't believe that Ashlynn and I had made a baby. That we were going to be parents.

Looking back up at her face, I smiled and cradling her face in my hands I kissed her. I swept my tongue along her lower lip and felt her arms reaching up and wrapping around me. I let go of her face and wrapped my arms around her waist and lifted her up onto me. Encompassing her legs around me, I walked into her apartment and shut the door behind me with my foot. I never took my mouth from hers as I walked us back to her room and slowly laid her down on the bed.

She giggled against my mouth and said, "I'm pregnant, Jason, I'm not dying."

Lifting myself off of her, I said, "I know you're pregnant—with my child."

Moving down her body, I lifted her t-shirt and kissed her stomach. She wrapped her fingers in my hair as I kissed all over her stomach and said, "I love you, little one. I love you so much." I then crawled back up Ash's body and said, "I'm so sorry, Ash. I love you so much."

Kissing me, she whispered against my mouth, "Then show me."

Getting onto my knees, I pulled Ash up with me and lifted her t-shirt up and over her. I then unclasped her bra and dropped it onto the floor. Placing her hands on the hem of my shirt, I lifted my arms as she pulled it off me. Pushing her back down to the bed, I kissed her, sucking her lower lip into my mouth and nibbling down on it. I rolled and pulled her nipples in between my fingers as she ran her hands up and down my back.

Breaking free of the kiss, I got up off the bed. Never taking my eyes off of Ash, I pushed my sweats and boxers down while she lifted her hips and took off her shorts and thong. Once all of our clothes were on the floor, I got back up on the bed and nestled in between her legs.

I started to a push a finger inside of her but she said, "Jason, I need you inside of me." Wrapping her legs around me, I pushed all the way inside her. We never took our eyes off one another as she gasped and I shuddered.

I don't think I'll ever get used to the fact that Ashlynn loves me and that our child is growing inside of her. It's an overwhelming experience and one I will certainly not mess up on.

I knew that I wasn't going to last long and just a few strokes in, I grunted, "I love you, Ash." Pulling my head down to hers, she kissed me and I thrust into her a few more times. We both fell over the edge into a state of bliss. As I kissed and sucked along her neck, she ran her fingertips up and down my back. Looking into her eyes, I kissed her and pulled out.

I got off her and laid on my side; she turned over to look at me with a smile on her face. Moving my hand up to her face, I stroked her cheek as I said, "I'm so sorry, Ash."

She smiled at me and said, "It's okay, Jason."

"No, it's not. I let the best the thing that's ever happened in my life leave and it took Jade slapping me and talking to me to fully realize that I make my own choices in life and I'm nothing like my dad."

Lifting her head to look at me, she said, "You are nothing like your dad, Jason."

"I know."

"Jade talked to you?"

I let out a laugh. "I know, right? Who would have thought that Jade was the one filled with all the wisdom? But I guess with all the mistakes she's made, she learns from them. So I guess it's a good thing."

Kissing me again, Ash said, "Be nice to your sister."

Wrapping Ash in my arms, I ran my hand up and down her back and for the first time in a really long time I was happy with my life. All of the reasons had Ashlynn Miller in them.

"What are you thinking about?" she asked.

"How happy I am right now and it's all because of you."

"I love you, Jason Williams."

"I'm in love with you, Ashlynn Miller," I said, pulling her on top of me.

After making love again, she lifted herself up off me and lay on her back. I don't even think she realized what she was doing but she was smiling as she slowly rubbed her stomach. For a couple of minutes, I just watched her and I couldn't wait to see our child grow inside of her. I also pictured a little girl who looked just like Ashlynn but caused a lot of trouble like me or a little boy who looked just like me but had a heart of gold like his mother.

"You're going to be a mom," I said.

She let out a laugh. "I know. I'm going to be a mom and you're going to be a dad."

Letting out a breath, I smiled because it just hit me. Kissing Ash on the lips. I looked into her eyes. "I'm going to be a dad."

Sucking in air, she said, "Now we just have to tell mine."

Chapter 14

Ashlynn

I couldn't believe how quickly Jason came around to me being pregnant with our child. It was all thanks to Jade. I don't know what I would have done if she wasn't there to help clean up the mess. Jade had really surprised me throughout the whole process, and I don't think I could ever thank her enough for bringing my Jason back to me. Jason wanted to tell everyone the second I was pregnant but I wanted to wait until the second trimester. I'd heard it was bad luck to tell earlier and I was scared something would happen to our little one. We compromised on two months later, when we would get our first ultrasound.

I couldn't wait to see my little peanut growing inside of my stomach. I knew I had to tell my dad soon but I wanted to have the ultrasound picture first. Jason surprised me big time after he came back around because he won't let me do anything.

It's already driving me crazy and I'm not even showing yet, but I love him so much.

We've been alternating between staying at each other's apartments but I know we're going to have to find a new place for us to live before our little peanut is born. I ended up staying at Jason's last night, so he drove me to the library and said he would be back at two for our doctor's appointment. The second I clocked out of work, I opened my phone to text him. As I exited the front doors of the library, I saw Jason leaning against the passenger door waiting for me.

Walking up to him, I kissed him on the cheek and he opened my door. He bowed low. "Your chariot awaits."

I just laughed at him. "Oh my god, you're ridiculous."

Leaning in to kiss me, he put a hand to my stomach. "I just don't want anything to happen to you or our little man."

"You don't know if our baby is a boy and we won't even find out until the second trimester," I said, giving him a quick kiss.

"Oh, I know it's a boy, Ash." Shaking my head I got into the car and buckled up as he closed the door.

The whole drive to the doctor's office Jason was acting so giddy. His leg was bouncing up and down and he was talking a mile a minute. He couldn't wait to see our baby on the sonogram machine and neither could I, but I was a little nervous about telling my dad that he was going to be a granddad. I was also scared for Jason's life because I didn't know how Daddy would react to it.

After we walked into the doctor's office and filled out all of the necessary forms, we were taken into a private room where we waited for the doctor. I sat down on the table and just watched Jason jumping up and down all over the place, full of adrenaline and excitement. I started laughing and then all of a sudden I got a little heartburn. I must have made a noise because Jason bolted over to me with a worried look on his face.

"Are you okay, Ash?" he asked, placing a hand on my stomach.

I kissed him on the cheek. "Relax Jason, everything is fine. I just have a little heartburn; nothing to worry about."

He shook his head like he understood but he was still biting his lower lip and I knew he was worried. I was just about to tell him to calm down when the doctor walked in and Jason started rambling to her about my heartburn. The doctor looked at me and just smiled.

"It's okay for her to have heartburn, Dad," she said, putting a reassuring hand on his shoulder.

The second he heard the word *dad,* his eyes twinkled and a big smile appeared on his face. Sitting down in a chair, Jason held my hand and rubbed lazy circles while the doctor talked to us about what we were to expect with the first trimester.

The doctor handed me a prescription for prenatal vitamins. "All right, now lie back down on the table and I'll show you your little bundle of joy on the machine."

I pulled my pants down on my hips so the doctor could apply some gel. Placing the wand low on my hips she moved it around for a bit and then we heard a heartbeat. Pointing to a little dot on the screen, the doctor said, "That right there is your baby."

Instantly tears formed in my eyes and I looked at Jason, who was staring at me with tears in his eyes. Standing up from his seat, he leaned in to me and kissed me on the lips. "I love you so much, Ash."

"I love you too, Jason."

"Do you guys want pictures?" asked the doctor.

Before I could even respond, Jason said, "Hell yeah, we want pictures!"

The doctor just laughed. "All right, Dad."

After flicking the lights back on, the doctor wiped the gel from my stomach and said she would be back with the pictures. As soon as the door closed behind her, Jason had me in his arms and he was kissing me. I entangled my arms around his waist and let my legs hang loose on either side of him as I bit down on his lip.

Gasping for air, Jason pulled back from me. "Behave, Ash." Kissing me once more on the lips, he sat down and we waited for our pictures to print. Once we got our pictures, we left the doctor's office. Getting back in the car, we started our four hour drive to my home. Daddy knew we were coming because I wanted to introduce him and Jason, but I was a nervous wreck about telling him that we were going to have a baby.

About an hour into our drive, Jason turned off the music and held onto my hand. Without taking his eyes off the road, he said, "It will be all right, Ashlynn."

Looking out the window, I took a deep breath. "I hope so."

***

Three hours later we were pulling into my driveway. I couldn't believe how long it had been since I was home. It seemed like forever ago and as nervous as I was to tell my dad our good news, I was ecstatic to see my dad because I really missed him.

I didn't even make it out of the car before my dad was opening the front door and running towards me screaming, "Ash!"

Picking me up and spinning me around, I could see the hesitation in Jason's face, but once I looked at him and mouthed, "I'm okay," he settled down.

Putting me back on my feet, Dad kissed me on the forehead and said, "I've missed you so much."

I wrapped my arms around his neck and kissed him on the cheek. "I've missed you so much."

Breaking eye contact, Dad looked over at Jason. Releasing me, he walked up to Jason. Jason extended his hand and said, "Nice to see you again, Mr. M—" but Dad cut him off.

Pointing a finger to Jason's chest he said, "I thought I told you to call me Garrett?"

Jason let out a forced laugh and said, "Sorry, Garrett, nice to see you again." Jason's hand was out towards Dad but Dad shrugged it off and pulled Jason into a hug.

I smiled at the two of them, amazed at how well they were both getting along, but I was still really nervous about telling Dad my news and how he would react to it. Picking up a bag, Dad slung an arm around me and then Jason took a hold of my other hand as we walked back to the house together. I wish I could have taken a photo of that image. I bet it was a beautiful one because I had the two men I loved most in the world by my sides.

Leaving our bags at the front door, I could smell seafood cooking and I asked, "Dad, what's the special occasion?"

Dad looked at me and said, "Well, as if it's not special enough that my daughter and her boyfriend came for a visit for the weekend, I have some news."

Taking a deep breath, I felt Jason tighten his hand around mine and I said, "I have some news, too."

Kissing me on the cheek, Dad said, "Well, all right, then. Ash, you'll be sleeping in your room."

Turning to Jason, he said, "You can take the spare room. Just a reminder; that room is right next to mine and I have exceptional hearing, so you might want to think before you do anything."

As soon as he said that, I yelled, "Dad!"

Turning to me, Dad shrugged his shoulders. "What?"

I was getting ready to yell at him but Jason put an arm over Dad's shoulder. "I thought you said you had exceptional hearing, Garrett?" I couldn't believe Jason said that—I just started laughing.

Dad laughed. "I have a feeling we'll get along just fine, smartass." Slapping Jason on the back, Dad walked into the kitchen and hollered, "Dinner should be ready soon, you two."

Carrying the bags upstairs, I showed Jason my room. It was the same way I had it in school. There were pictures all over the walls of friends, trophies from soccer, and my high school diploma.

Jumping onto my bed, he looked at all of the stuffed animals and then back at me. "Nice room, Ash."

Walking over and sitting down on his lap, I said, "Be nice. This was back in high school."

Chuckling, he pointed to the posters I had on the walls. "So, you don't listen to Justin Bieber music anymore?"

I shook my head. He continued, "So you don't like *Twilight* anymore?"

Shrugging his shoulders he said, "Then nothing's changed."

Taking his head in my hands and looking into his eyes, I said, "You're wrong because everything's changed."

Breaking eye contact, he looked down at my stomach and then back up at me. There were tears in his eyes. "I know." I quickly wiped them away and then kissed him with passion and love and understanding. I wanted to show him in that kiss that he meant everything to me in case he had any doubt.

"I love you so much, Ash."

"I love you, too."

We sat there in a comfortable silence for a couple of minutes and then heard the front door bell ring. I lifted my head from Jason's chest. "Are you expecting company?" he asked.

I shook my head back and forth but then I heard a woman's voice and Dad saying, "Hey."

My eyes widened, and looking over at Jason, he just shrugged his shoulders. "Well, I guess we found out your dad's news,"he said. Dad yelled up to us that dinner was ready.

Getting off Jason's lap, he kissed me on the forehead. "Like I said before, Ash, it will all be okay." Taking Jason's hand in mine, we walked down the stairs and I heard my dad and this lady having a conversation in the kitchen.

They must have heard our footsteps on the stairs because they stopped talking and Dad came out to meet us. "Ash, there's somebody I wanted you to meet." Behind him walked a short lady with blonde hair and brown eyes. I looked from her back to Dad. "This is Janie. We've been seeing each other for a while," he said.

My jaw dropped open and I looked between Dad and Janie in shock. Dad misunderstood my silence because he started rambling. "I'm sorry; I messed up, didn't I? It's just that you haven't been home in a while and I didn't want to tell you over the phone. I'm sor—"

Cutting Dad off, I took his hand in mine and said, "Can I talk to you in the other room, please?"

Dad slumped his shoulders and looked down at the floor, mumbling, "Yeah, Ash." Letting go of

Jason's hand, Dad and I walked into the den and sat down on the couch.

It was silent for a while and then Dad said, "I'm sorry; I didn't mean to spring this on yo—" Again I cut him off and hugged him. He flinched for a minute but then I felt his arms wrap around me.

Letting go of him, I said, "Daddy, I'm not mad at you for not telling me. It's just been a long time since Mom and I hated the fact that you were always alone. If you're happy, then I'm happy."

Dad had tears in his eyes and he quickly wiped them away. "Is it dusty in here, Ash, or what?"

I just laughed and kissed him on the cheek and said, "Come on, I'm starving." Grabbing Dad's hand, we walked back out into the front hall where Jason and Janie were standing awkwardly. The second Janie saw Dad, she smiled. I smiled and then looked over to Jason, who was staring at me in amazement and I winked at him.

Letting go of Dad's hand, I walked over to Janie and extended my hand. "I'm Ashlynn; it's nice to meet you, Janie."

Her smile got bigger and she extended her hand to me. "It's very nice to meet you, Ashlynn." Looking behind me, she said, "Your dad has told me so much about you."

After I introduced Jason to Janie, we all went into the kitchen and sat down at the table, where a huge pot of spicy shrimp with crunchy bread and salad were waiting for us. My mouth instantly watered and as soon as I sat down, I loaded my plate up with shrimp.

Dad got out a bottle of white wine and started pouring glasses but I startled and said, "Not me."

His back was to me but he turned around and said, "White wine is your favorite."

I looked to Jason for help and he quickly said, "I think Ash and I will just have water, Garrett."

I quickly let out the breath I was holding when I saw Janie looking between us from the corner of my eye. I looked at her and she picked up her hand and locked her lips when I mouthed, "Thank you." She nodded her head and we all went back to eating.

I must have been stuffing my face or something because I heard Dad laugh and say, "Jesus, Ash, are you eating for two?"

I started to choke and Jason began to pat my back.

Taking a sip of water, I wiped my mouth and looked over at Dad. "I'm just really hungry is all."

That's when Dad turned to Jason and asked, "Are you not feeding my girl?" Jason just started laughing.

After that little incident, dinner was a lot of fun. I found out that Janie was our new neighbor and she was a photographer. Her husband died of a brain tumor a couple of years back and they'd never had children but she told us all about her two little pugs named Ozzie and Allie who were a handful themselves.

Once dinner was over, Janie said she had to leave.

Shaking Jason's hand, she said, "Nice to meet you," and then walked over to me and pulled me into a hug and whispered, "Congratulations."

I whispered back, "Thank you," and she kissed me on the cheek.

Pulling away, my dad asked, "What were you ladies just whispering about?"

Looking back at me, Janie winked and then turned back to my dad. Kissing him on the lips, she said, "Nothing, Garrett, just girl stuff."

Jason walked over and placed an arm over my shoulder and muttered, "I like her."

With a smile on my face and not taking my eyes off my dad and Janie, I said, "Yeah, me too."

Taking Janie's hand, he turned back to me. "I'm going to walk Janie home but I want to hear all about your news when I get back."

Attempting to smile I said, "Okay, Daddy."

Without Dad's knowledge, Janie turned around and mouthed, "Good luck," while I mouthed, "I'll need it."

As soon as the door closed, I turned to Jason and he said, "Breathe, Ash, everything will be fine." He walked me over to the couch and we sat there in silence while we waited for Dad to come back.

Ten minutes later the front door opened and my heart jumped. Placing a hand on my thigh, Jason gave it a gentle squeeze and I looked over at him. He kissed me on the cheek. "I love you, Ash."

I smiled. "I love you, too."

Dad walked into the living room and plopped down in a chair. "So, what's going on?"

I looked to Jason and he just nodded his head. Turning to my dad, I said, "We're going to have a baby."

I was so scared that Dad was going to jump up from his seat and strangle Jason, but he did something worse. He just sat there in complete silence, looking between the two of us. Jason held tightly onto my hand and then Dad's vision stopped on Jason. "You still love my daughter?"

Jason cleared his throat and said, "More now, if that's possible."

Hunching forward in his chair, Dad asked, "That question you asked me over the ph—"

Jason cut him off. "It still stands, Mr. Miller."

Leaning back in his chair looking between the two of us for a solid minute, he said, "Well, okay then, and I thought I told you to call me Garrett."

Chuckling, Jason said, "Sorry, Garrett."

I'm sorry but was I living in the Twilight Zone *or something? My dad was acting like he was okay with it and I thought he was going to shit a brick or something.*

I needed to know what Dad was talking about with a question, but right now wasn't the time to do so. Looking over at Dad I asked, "You're not mad?"

Shaking his head back and forth, he said, "Ashlynn, you're twenty-one years old. I'm mad that I'm only forty-eight and that I'm going to be a grandpa, but we can't really do anything about that now, can we?"

Tearing up, I ran over to my dad and hugged him.

I hugged him because this could have gone down a completely different path.

Kissing him on the cheek, I leaned back and looked at him. He looked into my eyes and then looked down at my stomach and said, "My baby is going to have a baby." Placing a hand on my cheek, he wiped away my tears and got up and shook Jason's hand. Dad sat down on the couch with us but I jumped up and ran to get my purse.

I heard Dad ask Jason, "Where is she going?"

Jason laughed. "It's a surprise."

Getting my purse from the front hall, I walked back into the living room with the ultrasound and handed it to Dad. He took it from me and looked down and just started crying. Before I knew it, Jason and I were tearing up as well as we all stared at the picture of the little peanut growing inside of me.

The rest of the weekend went by faster than expected. We spent our time pulling out all of my baby clothes and looking through photo albums as Dad told us stories about me when I was little. We also visited Mom's grave, where I told her that I was going to have a baby and that she better look over our little one.

As much as I didn't want to leave, it was already Sunday, but as we were leaving my dad's house, I stopped on our walk to the car. Jason turned and tilted his head to the side because he didn't understand why I stopped.

Looking up at him, I asked, "What did you ask my dad on the phone when you first talked to him?"

Kissing me on the cheek, he looked into my eyes. "I'll tell you someday, I promise."

Chapter 15

Jason

I couldn't believe how fast the summer had gone and that we were all three weeks into our senior year of college. It was crazy that by the time we all graduated, Ashlynn and I would have a child. We found out that Ash was expected to deliver March 23rd.We calculated it when we got home that night and realized she got pregnant the first time she and I made love in the middle of June. Ash started showing a little bit but it wasn't enough that our friends would realize she was having a baby.

I was still pretty adamant that we were having a little boy, but it didn't matter to me as long as the baby and Ash were healthy. That was all that mattered in the end. I just had a feeling, and every time I rubbed her belly I said, "Little man."

She would laugh and shake her head, saying, "Or little girl."

A part of me kind of hoped we were having a boy because I knew that we would be in trouble when our little girl got older. With Ashlynn's looks, I knew without a doubt in my body I would have to deal with a bunch of little assholes and I wasn't ready for that. But today we were finally going to find out whether we were having a little girl or a little boy. The anticipation over this moment was driving me nuts and I knew I was driving Ashlynn nuts as well.

Pulling into the parking lot of the doctor's office, I opened Ash's door and held her hand as we walked into the building. Before walking into the office, I stopped and kissed Ash on the lips. "This is it."

Smiling up at me, she nodded. "Yeah, it is."

Giving our names, we sat in the waiting room, filled with anticipation to find out the gender of our little one. A nurse came out and asked, "Ashlynn Miller?"

We both jumped up and followed her into a room and then waited for the ultrasound tech to come in. I lifted Ash onto the table and she just laughed at me and said, "I'm fine, Jason," then kissed me on the lips.

Bouncing my knee up and down, I heard Ashlynn say, "Calm down, Jason."

I looked over at her and said, "I'm just really excit—" but was cut off when the doctor walked in and asked, "How are you feeling, Ashlynn?"

She started rubbing her stomach and said, "Fine, just get this one over here out of his misery and tell us what we're having, please."

191

The doctor looked over at me and said, "Excited, Jason?"

Standing up and taking Ash's hand in mine, I said, "Understatement of the year."

Turning on the machine, the doctor said, "All right, Ashlynn, you know the drill."

Ash laid back on the table and pulled down her pants, showing off her belly. I was surprised at how big Ash's belly was. She wasn't that far along, but I guess we were just going to have a big baby on our hands. After the doctor applied the gel and smoothed it out over Ash's stomach, she picked up the wand and began to move it around.

My heart was beating so fast and then the doctor pointed to the screen and said, "Congratulations, you guys are the proud parents of a little boy."

I wanted to jump up and down yelling, "Fuck yeah, I knew it!" Instead I looked over to Ash and winked at her while she shook her head. I leaned in to kiss her but the doctor said, "Wait; just a minute."

I stopped and looked over. "Is everything okay?"

The doctor let out a laugh and said, "Yeah, everything's fine, but you're having a girl."

Ashlynn looked over at me. "That's what I'm talking about."

That's when the doctor started waving her hand and said, "No. I mean you're having a little girl as well." I looked over at Ash and her eyes were huge.

Turning towards the doctor, we both talked over one another with Ash asking, "Come again?" and me asking, "I'm sorry, but what did you just say?"

The doctor turned to the both of us and said, "You're having a boy and a girl."

I still couldn't believe it so I asked, "We're having a twins?"

The doctor just laughed and said, "Yeah, that's what it's called when someone has two babies at the same time. Triplets are when someone has three."

I looked over to Ashlynn and just started laughing, saying, "Wow, when we mess up, *we mess up*." I tried to calm my laughter to look over at Ash but she still had this stunned look on her face.

Biting my laughter I asked, "Ash?"

That's when she turned to me and threw her head back and laughed.

Controlling our laughter, I leaned in and said, "I love you so much, Ash."

Cradling my face in her hands, she said, "I love you too, Jason."

Upon kissing her, we both turned to the doctor who was staring at us, probably thinking *These two are going to be parents? That's a little frightening.*

After getting our pictures from the ultrasound, I drove us back to my apartment. I was so excited that we could finally tell all of our friends. Sarah, Gabe, Ryder, Isabelle, Patrick, and for some dumbass reason, Ashlynn wanted to invite Derrick. I didn't put too much of a fight into it because I wanted Ash to be happy, and plus, he seemed like an okay guy if I didn't include the fact that he'd touched her and probably kissed her. Jade and Neil would be at the party as well. They already knew about the pregnancy but they didn't about the gender, or genders. We decided we were going to throw a party to celebrate that we were all seniors, but little did they know that both Ashlynn and I had a little surprise on our hands. *Or should I say little surprises?*

Everybody already knew about the party because we wanted to hold it the day we found out about the gender of our child. We also wanted to wait to get the okay from the doctor to start telling people in case something happened. We decided for the party to just be casual, so while Ashlynn took a nap in my room, I cleaned up the house, then ordered and picked up pizzas. I also made a run to the liquor store, picking up beer and champagne for the news, and stopped at the grocery store to pick up some more ginger ale for Ash as well as sparkling cider.

By the time I got back from running the errands, Ash was waking up and walking out into the living room. As she was stretching, her t-shirt rolled up and I caught a glimpse of her little belly.

Yawning, she looked at me and asked, "What's that look for?"

Placing the pizzas on the counter, I walked over to her. "You think we have time before everybody starts showing up for the party?"

Lifting her into my arms, she giggled. Wrapping her legs around me, she whispered, "We have all the time in the world," before capturing her mouth with mine.

***

As soon as everyone arrived, we started hanging out and having a good time. Joking around and talking about what we did over the summer. How classes were going and how we just couldn't wait to graduate this year. We had music playing and the drinks were flowing as we munched on chips and ate pizza. It was an all around good time but I couldn't wait to tell everyone our great news.

Halfway through the night, I said, "All right everyone, go sit down in the living room. Ash and I have something to tell you." I looked over at Jade and saw a little smile creep onto her face. I just couldn't wait to see her face when I told them we were having twins.

With drinks and pizza in hand, everyone gathered in the living room and waited for Ashlynn and I to share our news. Once everyone sat down, Ash and I looked at one another and smiled. We looked out at everyone and then Sarah said, "I'm going crazy; just tell us already! The anticipation is killing me."

Everyone started laughing and as soon as the laughter died down, I screamed, "Ash is pregnant!"

I don't think I've ever seen that many mouths fall open and eyes get wide in one place but it scared the shit out of me. All the girls started screaming for joy and the guys said, "Congrats," but I put my hand up and said, "That's not the best part."

Jade looked between Ash and I and asked, "What's the best part?"

I looked over at Ashlynn and she looked out at everyone.

With a big smile on her face she said, "We're having a boy." She paused for a second. "And a girl."

Everyone was loud but then Jade jumped up and said, "Well, shit, motherfuckers! When you guys go big, you seriously go big."

All of the girls, as well as Patrick, ran over to Ashlynn to touch her stomach while the guys walked over to me and shook my hand or patted me on the back. Honestly, I tried to stay in the conversation they were having, but I couldn't keep my eyes off Ashlynn. She really was something and she wore that pregnancy glow well. She was rubbing her stomach and laughing at everything Jade, Isabelle, Sarah, and Patrick had to say.

A little while later as I was showing everyone the pictures of the sonograms, the telephone rang. Ash was closest to it, so she answered the phone and her facial expression changed within an instant. She went from smiling to turning as pale as a ghost and her eyes bugged out of her head. Not taking my eyes off her, I said, "Quiet, guys, Ash is on the phone."

I heard her say, "Okay, bye."

Walking over to her, I put my hands on her shoulders.

"Jason," she said. She searched for my sister. "Jade. Your dad was just admitted into the hospital and they don't know how long he has."

Turning towards Jade, she had tears in her eyes and I didn't even have to tell everyone the party was over. Everyone gave us hugs and said they would be here for us when we got back.

Once everyone left, Ashlynn, Jade, Neil, and I got into the car and drove to the hospital. Over the last two months, Neil and Jade had formed a friendship and I knew she needed someone to lean on during this time at the hospital, so I asked him if he would come with us. I didn't really have to twist his arm too much.

"I'll drive," he offered.

Walking into the hospital, I felt dread come over me. I honestly didn't understand why I was here except for the sole fact that Jade wanted to be here. We walked up to the receptionist's desk and the lady sitting there and asked, "How can I help you?"

Letting out a breath, I said, "We're here to see Benjamin Williams."

Looking at her computer, she typed in a few things. "He's in room 312." Pointing behind us, she said, "Take the elevator to the third floor and you will find it with no problem."

I nodded. "Thank you."

We all turned around and walked over to the elevator. Once it opened, I pressed the button for the third floor and the doors closed behind us. Ashlynn moved closer to me and wrapped her hand in mine. I looked over at her and she gave a small smile in reassurance. She was letting me know that she was here for me. I then looked over towards Jade and saw that Neil had an arm over her, whispering things into her ear and I was happy that someone was comforting my sister.

When the elevator doors opened to the third floor, we turned left and walked to room 312. I put my hand to the knob and could feel my hand shaking. I took a step back. "I can't do this," I said, and let go of Ash's hand and went to sit in the waiting room.

What was I supposed to say to someone who beat the shit out of me when I was little and messed up mine and Jade's adult lives? I had no fucking clue. I didn't even know where to start and the man was dying literally ten feet away from me.

I heard Ash say something to Neil and Jade. Once they opened the door and walked into the room, she turned and walked straight towards me. Sitting down in a chair next to me, she took my hand in hers and started rubbing her thumb back and forth. I was so ashamed. "I can't do this, Ash."

Placing a hand on the side of my face, she turned my head so I was looking at her. Tears started pouring from my eyes and she got up from her chair and sat down on my lap. I buried my face in her neck and sobbed while she rubbed up and down my back and whispered in my ear. She told me that it was okay to cry and how much she loved me.

Gathering myself, I looked up at her. "I love you so much, Ashlynn."

She kissed me on the cheek. "I know, Jason."

Standing from my lap, she sat back down in the chair and looked towards my dad's room and started talking. "That man messed up yours and Jade's childhoods beyond repair and you both are here at the hospital while he is dying. The both of you are such strong people and I am proud to say that Jade is my best friend."

Turning to me, she placed a hand to her stomach and said, "And I have no words to describe the adoration, respect, and love I feel for you, Jason Williams. I'm left speechless. Whatever choice you make, I will stand by you and respect it … but I do think you need closure. I don't want you going through life thinking about the what-if's if you don't walk in that room and confront him or tell him how you feel." She pointed towards room 312. "And you don't have much time to find that closure."

This is one of the many reasons why I loved Ashlynn Miller, because she told me exactly what I needed to hear when others were sometimes too afraid to say it to my face.

A couple of minutes later, Neil walked out with Jade wrapped in his arms while she cried. She was so broken up that halfway to the waiting room, Neil lifted my sister into his arms and cradled her. He walked over and sat in a chair, smoothing her hair back away from her face. Looking over at Ashlynn, I nodded my head and we both got up and walked towards room 312. This time when I placed my hand on the knob, I took a deep breath and walked in, closing the door behind us.

The room was dark with a bunch of machines all over the place. There were monitors and sounds beeping and signaling the morphine drip. I looked around the room and my eyes stopped on the man lying in the bed with his eyes closed with an oxygen mask around his face. He looked so fragile and weak and I started to choke up. Walking over to the side of his bed, there were two chairs available and I took the one closest to him so I could release everything I had built up for twenty-one years of my life.

Ashlynn sat next to me and never let go of my hand as I vented and he never opened his eyes.

It didn't matter to me if he was awake or asleep. The only thing that mattered to me was that I had finally told this man how badly he messed up. Not only his relationship with his children but our own relationships as people.

Leaning towards him, I said, "You messed me and Jade up completely. We had childhoods that no one should have to go through and because of you I have lived my life up until recently angry with myself. Angry with how I let you get to me. I let you get into my head and mess up any opportunity I ever had. I always had your voice in the back of my head saying that I would never be good enough and that I was not worthy of love. But guess what? You were wrong."

I pointed to Ash. "I fell in love with this girl a long time ago and I didn't want to mess up with her the way you and Mom messed Jade and I up. So do you want to know what I did? I pushed her away and slowly but surely with tiny baby steps she broke down my walls. She has shown me what love means and what it really is. I'm so grateful to have her in my life. Another thing you should know is that she's pregnant with my children. We're having twins, a boy and a girl, and unlike you, I will love them unconditionally. I will build them up instead of tear them down. I will cheer them on instead of break them apart. I will hug and kiss them rather than hit them.

"I will tell you this, though. The second she told me she was pregnant I was scared out of my mind that I would become like you, but I've realized that I make my own choices in life and after today I will never have your voice in my head telling me how royally I messed up and how I failed because the only failure I see … is you."

Closing my eyes and opening them, tears rolled down my face. Quickly wiping them away, I got up from my chair and leaned into his ear so he could hear me. "I forgive you," I whispered. Those three words had his eyes opening up and I realized he was tearing up.

Barely lifting his hand, I looked down at it and placed my hand in his. I looked back up into his eyes as he pulled the oxygen mask from his face and taking a deep breath, he wheezed out, "I'm so sorry, Jason."

I didn't realize that his apology was what I needed to hear to be okay. Leaning in, I kissed him on the forehead and whispered, "You can go now, Dad." Sitting back down in the chair, I never took my eyes away from his face as his eyes closed for the last time and the monitor line went straight and a buzz went off.

Taking a deep breath, I looked over to see Ashlynn with tears streaming down her face. I got up from my chair and pulled her into my chest and hugged her. That hug represented how grateful I was to have her in my life and the relief that washed over me after forgiving my dad. Kissing her on the top of the head, I placed an arm around her and we walked out of the room into the waiting room where Neil was still holding Jade.

Lifting her head from Neil's chest, she looked over towards me and I shook my head. Getting up from Neil's lap, she ran over to me and I wrapped my arms around her. Calming her down, Neil walked up behind her and wrapped his arms around her. I wrapped my arm around Ashlynn, kissing her on the forehead.

Turning back to Neil and Jade, I said, "Let's go home."

Chapter 16

Ashlynn

We were now in the month of December and it had been four months to the day since Jade and Jason's dad passed away. I was also in my third trimester and doing rather well. Sitting in that hospital room with him as Jason poured out his soul to his dad was heartbreaking but I was so proud of him for talking to his dad and telling him how he felt. I knew he'd needed that closure and I just did not want him to have to go through life thinking about how he would regret not taking the opportunity to let it all out there.

Jade and Jason decided not to go to the funeral because all they really needed was to have some peace of mind and find some closure with their father. However, a month after Ben Williams' death, Jade and Jason both received letters in the mail informing them that their dad was leaving them each a large sum of money. Jason wouldn't tell me the exact amount and I wasn't comfortable asking, but he told me that it was enough to live comfortably with the twins.

That first month after Jason's dad's death was rather difficult on him and I did not expect that. While he did get his closure at the hospital, it all seemed to go downhill from there. He started thinking about contacting his mom but opted against it. He said he didn't want to drag that mess into our lives when we were just getting used to it.

I also didn't expect to see Jade and Neil becoming so close. He really took care of her after their dad's death and I was so happy. I just hoped that she didn't make a mistake with Neil because I could see their friendship growing into something.

T I decided to take my last semester of college online because I was in my third trimester. It would be pretty difficult to fit into the desks and sit comfortably with my growing belly.

Explaining the whole taking my courses online to my dad was hard. He wasn't too pleased but said that he was so proud of me either way, because I was going to graduate college. He was also ecstatic about Jason and I having twins and said he couldn't wait to spoil them rotten. I remember having the conversation with him after Jason's dad's death and he said that maybe it was a sign from above that we were given both a little girl and a little boy. One to represent my mom and the other Jason's dad.

I told Jason what my dad said and he smiled. and said, "Yeah, maybe he's right," he said. I like to think that maybe my dad was right and it got me thinking about what we were going to name our children but I just wanted to run it by Jason to see if he was comfortable with it.

Jason and I had made plans to move in together and since Jade was going to have an extra room, she offered to let Neil move in with her. Of course he jumped on that option because anyone who looked at them could see that they had chemistry.

After a ton of begging on Neil's side, Jason caved, saying, "It's fine by me but make one mistake and we will have problems." Neil promised Jason but I knew he probably had his fingers crossed behind his back while he shook Jason's hand.

I thought it was really cute how Jason looked after Jade and I couldn't wait to see our children grow up and see them treat one another that way. I was an only child, so I never got to experience the whole sibling thing. I didn't have to share my toys and I pretty much got anything I ever wanted. But I also missed out on a lot. I didn't always have someone to play with or talk to. I had to find my own ways to keep myself occupied which is why sometimes I think I read so many books. *Yes, read as in past tense.*

I wasn't really reading books that much anymore because I didn't have a reason to have to escape from my real life anymore because I had Jason. We found one another. Although I will mention that I did read Isabelle's book, *Ours*. Iz asked for Sarah, Jade and I to read her book before she sent it off to publishing houses. She thought about self-publishing but her dream was to be signed by a huge publishing house. Needless to say, it was amazing but I knew right away that it was about her and Ryder. From the first page I knew and I couldn't wait for her to write the next book in the series.

We all decided that over Winter Break I was going to move into Jason's apartment and Neil would move into Jade's. *I know, stupid, right? I mean we live in Maryland where it snows like a motherfucker and our brilliant plan is to move over Christmas break. Yeah, don't tell me because I already know we are all dumbasses.*

But that's exactly what we all did. Of course Jason wouldn't let me help move anything because I was six months pregnant, so I got to unpack my clothes and put them away in Jason's closet and drawers. I couldn't believe where my life had led me and how quickly everything had changed. It felt like sometimes we were literally on a roller coaster ride with the ups and downs in our relationship. Jason always referred to our moments of peace and serenity as beautiful and the rough and difficult times as a mess. So it literally went mess, beautiful, mess, beautiful, mess … beautiful but it was mine and Jason's, so I wouldn't complain about anything.

We had just finished moving me into Jason's apartment and Neil into Jade's. I was folding my clothes on Jason's chest of drawers when he walked up and wrapped his arms around me, resting them on my belly. I leaned back against him. "How are my girls and little boy doing today?" he asked.

The second he finished asking the question, our little ones started rolling around in my belly and

Jason could feel them kicking. He started laughing; I could feel him against my back.

Turning my head, I looked up at him and said, "My answer good enough for you?"

Turning me around so I was facing him, he wrapped his arms around me. "I love you, Ashlynn. Welcome home." He started to lean in to kiss me but I pushed him away from me and started walking backwards toward the bed.

Without taking my eyes from Jason, I pulled my sweatshirt off and unclasped my bra and let them fall to the floor. Leaning forward, I took off my yoga pants and thong and sat down on the edge of the bed. Scooting backwards, I said, "We have to christen the bedroom. It's tradition, you know?"

Taking his jacket off and dropping it to the floor, he quickly took off his shirt as well. Unclasping the belt from his jeans, he unbuttoned and pushed down his jeans and boxers. My mouth watered as I saw Jason was up and ready for me and if I wasn't wet before, I was now. Jason walked up to the edge of the bed, and wrapping his hands around my ankles, gently pulled me to the edge. Looking down at me, he said, "Spread your legs, Ashlynn." I did as he said and he trailed his fingers up my right thigh and slowly pushed two fingers inside me.

I gasped and he hissed through his teeth because he felt how wet I was for him. As he pushed his two fingers in and out of me, I reached out and stroked him at the same tempo. It was slow and meticulous because Jason wanted to drag it out. Of course I loved when we fucked but these were the times I enjoyed most because we made it last longer and longer each time. Jason loved getting me to the brink of ecstasy and slowly letting me fall back down. He thought it was hilarious and loved hearing me scream, "Just fuck me, Jason!"

Releasing my hand from around Jason, I took the hand that had the fingers inside me and slowly slid them out.

Pushing him back a little, I got up off the bed and turned us so he was sitting down. Leaning in to his ear, I whispered, "Move back, Jason, and sit up."

Moving back to the wall, he sat there and waited for me with anticipation in his eyes. I crawled up the bed and rested between his legs while his cock was pushed up against my swollen belly. Lifting up, Jason held himself still and I sank down onto him.

Being on top with Jason was a breathtaking experience. He filled me completely; almost like he was made for me, and in a sense I guess he was. As a matter of fact, I knew he was. Wrapping his arms around me, I put my hands on his shoulders and slowly moved up and down him because I wanted to drag this out as long as possible.

We whispered little things back and forth to one another. Jason telling me how much he loved me. Me telling him how much I cherished him. Torturously slowly we both brought ourselves over the edge. Me pulling Jason inside of me even deeper as he released inside of me.

It was times I enjoyed the most because when we both finished, I said, "I love you, Jason," and he would grunt, "I love you so much, Ashlynn."

He rarely ever used my nickname anymore, which I found downright sexy. I asked him about it once and he said, "I called you Ash when we were friends."

With a smirk on his face and love in his eyes he said, "We're not friends anymore. We became best friends who fell in love with one another."

We both decided that for Christmas this year we would just buy things we needed for the twins and one present for each other. Jason didn't like it because he said he wanted to spoil me rotten but I didn't want to be spoiled, I just wanted his love and I got it. So whatever else came out of us was extra. A bonus, if you will, because I had already won the ultimate prize: Jason Thomas Williams.

Over the course of the week of Christmas we got cribs, a changing table, dressers, clothes, and a baby bag, tons of diapers, a double stroller, and car seats. I couldn't believe how much money we had spent and I tried to tell Jason that I had money to help pay for it but he waved me off and said to not worry about it.

Decorating the twins' room was the best part. I painted the walls, half being blue with fish swimming all over the place while the other half was pink with ballet shoes and tiaras. Art was always a passion of mine so I enjoyed decorating our children's room while Jason yelled and screamed having to set up the cribs. Of course, being Jason, he thought he could do it without having to read the instructions, so it took him probably three times as long to set them up as if he had read the instructions. We stocked their dressers to the brim with clothes that would probably last a month if we were lucky. On my own I bought our little boy a pair of navy Converse and our little girl a pair of chestnut UGG boots. They were just so adorable I had to get them.

We were at the mall when I got them and was so excited to show Jason while he got a gift for me. Jason just laughed at me and said, "As long as you're happy, Ashlynn, then that's all that matters."

I shook my head and said, "No, your happiness matters as well, Jason."

Stopping mid-step, he turned, wrapped his arms around me, and kissed me. Leaning away from me to look into my eyes, he said, "I can't not be happy when I'm with you."

***

Today was Christmas Eve and we decided to just lounge around finishing up decorations and whatnot before the babies arrived. We also watched *A Christmas Story,* maybe four times. I also packed overnight bags for the delivery because we just needed to be prepared. I would rather be overprepared than underprepared.

Later in the night, Jason decided to surprise me with a picnic in the living room. He had all of my favorite foods lying on the floor. Pickles (Pregnant here. Remember?), chips and salsa, yogurt, cheese and crackers, mango slices, and celery with peanut butter. He also made himself a sandwich and had some sparkling cider in glasses for us.

I was busy dipping a mango slice into some yogurt when Jason said, "Can you believe that next year we'll be celebrating Christmas with our kids?"

Leaving the mango slice in the yogurt, I crawled over to Jason and kissed him. I couldn't believe how lucky I was to have him. Crawling back over to my seat, I grabbed the mango slice and just as I was about to put it in my mouth, I looked up and caught Jason staring at me.

Waving the yogurt covered mango in the air, I said, "What?"

"I just love you so much."

Leaning over I said, "I love you, too," and kissed him. Finally getting to eat, he went back to his sandwich. Swallowing my bite, I said, "Jason?"

He looked over at me and around a mouthful, said, "Yeah?"

"I have two names I picked out and I wanted to see what you thought of them."

Placing the sandwich on a napkin, he took a sip of his drink. "Ashlynn, whatever you pick, I'll love."

I smiled. *Okay, here goes nothing.* "I combined our names, so I thought for a little girl we would name her Jaylin. For our little boy, I thought Bennett. For that I combined my mom's name Annette and your dad's name Benjamin."

Closing his eyes, he let out a breath. I thought he was pissed at me for bringing his dad into the name of our son, so I quickly said, "We don't have to—" but he cut me off and leaned over.

He cupped my face in his hand. "Thank you," he said, and kissed me. After that we forgot all about the food on the floor as he carried me back to our room and we made love.

The day of Christmas, Jason and I spent our time in bed, talking and laughing. We also cuddled, kissed, and made love. Of course he surprised me with waffles with syrup and hot chocolate like our first time together. Unlike our first time, I refused to share with him so he had to get his own plate. Neither of us wanted to cook anything, so we ordered Chinese food and had another picnic in the living room and it was the best Christmas I have ever had so far.

We decided to exchange our gifts during dinner. Jason got me a spa package to get a massage, manicure, pedicure, facial, and my hair done before the babies were born. He also got me some comfy socks and slippers because I always complained about my feet hurting.

I was so nervous to give him mine. I didn't spend a lot of money on it but I wanted it to come from the heart. I gave him a huge basket and filled it with little things he loved like licorice and Tootsie Roll pops. I also put in a case of his favorite beer and t-shirts and sweatpants he wanted, but the most important part was a photo album I made for him. Jade had taken a picture of us together our freshman year of college. She said she wanted to have a picture of the two people she loved the most. Little did she know that three years later those two people would fall in love.

The picture wasn't anything special. It was taken a night we were all studying in mine and Jade's room. Jason and I were in an art class together and I was helping him study for a test we were having. Jade was doing homework for a business course she was enrolled in at the time. The three of us were also drinking, so Jason and I didn't get a lot of studying done, but somehow we both aced the test. I guess there really is logic in mixing together drinking alcohol and late night cram sessions.

Anyway, Jason and I were both in sweats and he was making a joke and I was laughing because it was funny. I would have probably laughed either way. There was a second where we both looked at one another and that's when Jade took the photo. I placed it in the front of the album and across the bottom it had one word … memories. On the inside cover I wrote Jason a note that I wanted him to remember for the rest of our lives together.

Dear Jason,

I can't believe how quickly everything has changed for us. You joke all the time about me being beautiful and you being a mess but really it's the opposite. You are the most beautiful person I have ever known and will without a doubt in my mind, ever know, both on the inside and the out. I can't wait to spend the rest of my life with you raising Jaylin and Bennett, watching them grow and become beautiful little messes of their own.

I knew the day I met you that you were it for me. You stole my heart move-in day freshman year of college and I now know that I stole yours, I just wasn't aware of it back then. I can't wait to see where my life takes me and I know I will be happy because I'll have you by my side. After all, I'm the

beautiful to your mess. This is the first of many albums to fill with all of the memories we have and will share together and I can't wait to fill them up with you. I love you, Jason Williams.
Forever Yours,
Ashlynn

I don't think I had ever seen Jason cry so much in my life as he read the letter and looked at all of the photos I picked out to put in it. I had put baby pictures of Jason and I in the album, along with a few when we were little, our senior pictures, and some from our time in college together. Then I put the first and second sonogram pictures in there. Finally, the last was a picture Jade had also taken of me and Jason on move-in day to his apartment.

We had all just finished moving into our new apartments and Jason had walked up behind me and placed both his hands on my stomach. I smiled and placed my hands on top of his and turned my head to kiss when the flash went off.

We'd both then looked over at Jade who had tears in her eyes as she looked at us and said, "You're no longer a mess."

Chapter 17

Ashlynn

Two weeks have gone by since Christmas and Jason and I have fallen more in love, if it's even possible. We have fallen over the edge. We have fallen into oblivion and I hope we never get out. I had texted Jade because school was about to start and I had accidentally left a few things at her apartment.

God that feels weird now, calling the apartment hers instead of ours. We had shared some great memories in that little piece of crap. I was in another hole in the wall now but I was with the man I loved and that is where we were going to start our family and I couldn't wait.

I remember moving in freshman year of college and after meeting Jason, then Jade came running out. I just remember looking at her and thinking that it was a mistake we were put together as roommates. She looked like the complete opposite of me. I was so simple and plain. I was ordinary. I read books and I had never gotten into any sorts of trouble growing up. Jade, on the other hand, was always getting into mischief and making mistakes. Sometimes I envied her but other times I'd wondered what had happened to mess her up so much.

While I do think part of her attitude towards relationships was built on her childhood with Jason and having to deal with their mother and father, I knew that wasn't the whole story. Though she never told me, I had a feeling it had to do with the first boy she ever fell in love with. Sometimes I wondered if I had made a mistake never asking her but I thought maybe she would open up to me, but that never was the case.

Finding out everything that happened to Jade and Jason, it gave me a little more insight on them and I just hoped one day Jade would find someone who would make her the way Jason makes me feel. Happy and alive. Able to breathe when you feel like you're suffocating. Feeling like you can do anything and be anything because this person loves you. This is what I thought about as I drove to Jade's apartment, but when I got out of my car and walked up to the apartment, I looked at it. Really looked at it. I took in the brown shutters, red door, and the welcome mat outside the door. I looked at the doorbell that still didn't work, even after living there for two years.

We moved into that apartment and quickly made it our home. Sure, in the beginning we complained about the drippy faucet, the toilet that didn't always flush, and how we had to hurry in order to get a hot shower. However we decorated and hung pictures on the wall that we had taken freshman year of college. We made dinner and ate at the dining room table. Now granted, most of our dinners consisted of ramen noodles and easy mac and cheese, but in the end it was the company, more or less.

We filled our home with memories of staying up till three in the morning watching chick flicks and eating ice cream. We got drunk and made fools of ourselves as we danced around to N*Sync and the Backstreet Boys, screaming at the top of our lungs, "I want it that way," only to have mere minutes go before the neighbors banged on our door complaining about the loud ruckus.

Standing at the door, I also remembered my time with Jason. While I had moved into his apartment to begin our family, I looked beyond the door at Jade's apartment and remembered that this was where we had made it. It was where my life had completely changed. I never thought packing my bag to go to Vegas for Isabelle's birthday and Sarah and Gabe's wedding party would completely flip my life upside down.

Make me dizzy and giddy.

Make me cry and beg and plead.

Make me realize who I am.

I quickly wiped away my tears and pulled out my key because Jade told me to keep a key and for Neil to keep a key to mine and Jason's apartment in case we ever needed anything. This was the first time that I had been to the apartment since I moved out over three weeks ago and it felt like everything had changed. I guess it had. While Jade and I would always keep our best friend status, we were both moving in two different directions.

I mean shit. I was pregnant with twins and Jade was still Jade, I just hoped and prayed not for long. Opening the door, I saw the box Jade had left me on the kitchen island. Walking in and closing the door behind me, I started to walk over to the box when I heard moaning and grunting. I stopped dead in my tracks because I couldn't believe what I was hearing.

"Oh god, Neil."

"You feel so good, baby."

"Neil. Oh god, Neil."

"Ah, Jade."

Wait a minute did I just hear Jade's name?

"God, Jade. Jade."

Well, then, I guess that answers that question.

I started walking backwards. I figured I could just run out of here but I was almost seven months pregnant, so the chances of that happening were pretty slim. I decided to just leave the box and come back later. Hopefully when neither of them was there. I had just made it to the door when Neil's door opened and Jade walked out in his t-shirt.

Her back was to me and she said, "I'll be back for round two in a minute."

Giggling at him, she started to turn around as I was twisting the knob and then we both froze.

"Ashlynn!"

I knew my face was bright red and I had no clue what to do. I thought about running out of there but again, seven months pregnant. Instead I dropped my hand from the door and said, "Um?" Her mouth was wide open and I was caught in headlights. Shaking off my nerves I said, "Um, I came to get that box of stuff I left here." She still looked really stunned but then all of a sudden I started to think about it.

Even though I only saw friendship with Neil, I knew he deserved to be treated right. From what I gathered, he didn't seem like the type of guy to just have sex with a girl once. He seemed like the type of guy who made love and fucked every once in a while.

Leaning my back against the door, I said, "Please tell me, Jade, what the hell is going on?"

"I'm just going to go and get Neil," she said.

"I don't want to talk to Neil. I want to talk to my best friend. I want to know what the hell is going on here," I said.

She bit her lip. "I'm just going to go get some sweats on and I'll be back." Turning away from me, she went into her room and I walked over to the couch.

My heart was beating so fast as I pulled a blanket onto my lap. I just didn't know what the fuck to do. I mean Jade was my best friend and Jason was my boyfriend. Fuck, we were starting a family together and I didn't want to keep this secret from him.

I was having this mental conversation with myself when Jade walked back out into the living room and sat down on the couch. Two cushions away from me.

Laughing, I said, "Jade, I don't hate you but I just don't want you to make another mistake. I want my best friend to find what I have with her brother, that's all. So if this is—"

"Wow, let's rewind, Ash, and I'll explain everything to you, okay?"

Nodding, she began to explain what happened here.

Looking back at Neil's room, my old room, she said, "You've seen him and he's extremely good looking. Just seeing that eyebrow ring makes me go bananas."

Raising my eyebrows, she waved her hand in front of her face and said, "Anyway, he really took care of me after Dad passed away. I was just so torn up over what happened and I started to lean on Neil. We talked a lot and grew close to one another. I guess you could say that we formed a friendship and I felt comfortable with him."

After he moved in, we got closer and one night…" Waving her hand in the air, she shook her head. "I know you're probably going to think it was a big mistake, but we decided to be a sort of friends with benefits."

Mouth hanging open, I looked at her. "Jade, I will love you for as long as I live. I mean, for fuck's sake, you are my best friend and I know that I'm yours. So, as your best friend, I will tell you that this is a big mistake. You guys are fucking roommates for hellfire. I mean, were you really not thinking when you had this brilliant plan?"

I felt so bad, because next thing I knew, she was tearing up. Getting up from my seat, I walked over and sat next to her. I wrapped her up in my arms and pulled her as close to me as my seven months' pregnant belly would allow.

Kissing her on the top of her head, I rubbed up and down her back and whispered, "I'm so sorry, Jade. I didn't mean for it to come out bitchy. But you're the sister I never had and I'm trying to look out for you. I'm not saying that Neil is a bad guy, because from what I know of him, he's really nice. But Jade, did you not think about the consequences to your actions? Did you not think that this could be a big mistake?"

Lifting her head from my shoulder and releasing her arms from around me, she wiped away her tears and sniffled. Slumping her head, she said, "For the longest time I didn't think I would ever get what you and Jason have. But—"

"But?"

Sucking in a breath, Jade whispered, "But with Neil I have it. I fell in love with him, Ash."

It was now my turn to suck in a breath. With tears forming in my eyes, I said, "He's it?"

Nodding her head slightly, she looked at me and whispered, "Yes."

A small smile appeared on my face. I was so happy for Jade, but then my smile disappeared because of something. Or should I say someone.

Opening my mouth I uttered, "We have to tell Jason."

Immediately shaking her head, Jade jumped up from the couch and said, "No, please Ash! Please don't tell him!"

Shaking my head back and forth I said, "I can't lie to him, Ash."

With tears falling from her face, Jade whispered, "Please, don't tell him, Ash. For once I'm happy and I just want to enjoy it for a little while before it all goes to hell. Because you know Jason will get pissed off and start something with Neil."

Letting my head fall backwards and land on the couch, I closed my eyes. "This is a big mistake, Jade." Lifting my head up, I looked at her. "You know that, right?"

With a small smile on her face, she shook her head. "I don't care because I've learned that every mistake I've ever made has taught me a lesson in one way or another."

"I'm giving you until graduation, Jade."

Closing her eyes, Jade nodded her head. Slowly opening her eyes, I saw unshed tears in them. Before I could contemplate it, Jade wrapped her arms around my neck and hugged me.

Wrapping my arms around her waist, I whispered in her ear, "I love you, Jade."

Nodding her head in the crook of my neck, she kissed it and whispered, "Right back atcha."

Holding onto each other for a few seconds, we released and sat back on the couch. I watched as Jade looked down at her intertwined fingers and smiled. In turn, I smiled but I wondered what would happen when Jason found out just exactly what his sister was up to.

***

Two months have gone by since school has started and I'm doing great. I thought online classes would be a piece of cake, but they are actually really difficult. I have to write a lot of papers and there are a ton of group discussion chat forums I have to do a week. I no longer work at the library because it was just too much on my poor swollen ankles. I'm now eight and a half months pregnant and it's March 12th. It's a rather difficult day because this was the day my mom was born and I kept tearing up because I miss her so much.

Calling my dad, I cried and told him about how much I missed Mom and how I wish she was going to be here for the birth of Jaylin and Bennett. Dad did something unexpected and laughed. He said, "Ashlynn, your mother will be there with you every step of the way, whether you can see her or not."

Smiling through the phone, I told him that I loved him and I would see him in a week, then hung up.

Dad and Janie were going to be staying in a hotel for a week and helping Jason and I with the twins. Those little lovebirds were still going strong and I saw wedding bells in their future. I was just so happy that Dad had found someone because over the years, I worried about him living in the house all by himself.

As soon as I hung up the phone, I went back to our room to take a nap. Before lying down on the bed, I looked at the calendar. Jason and I were counting down the days until we got to finally see Jaylin and Bennett. We can't wait to hold them in our arms and watch them grow right in front of our eyes into amazing, beautiful people. I'm also excited to finally be able to sleep again. The little troublemakers move around all night long so I don't really get a lot of sleep. Just a ton of cat naps here and there.

I have totally given up reading romance books and have filled my Kindle shelf with baby books instead. Jason and I read together at night about anything and everything baby related. He loves laying on his side and resting his head on my stomach. He gets a kick out of feeling the little ones kick in my stomach. While he finds it to be the coolest thing ever, I find it rather uncomfortable now.

I remember the first time I felt the babies kick.

***

While Jason cooked dinner for the two of us, I sat in the living room reading a baby book. I was maybe four months along,. before we even found out we were having twins. *You think we would have recognized it then that we were having twins? Apparently not.*

As I took notes on the growth of our baby, I felt butterflies in my stomach. Something more than butterflies. Placing the baby book on the seat next to me, I felt it again. I groaned.

"Ash, are you okay?" Jason panicked as he dropped the spatula and ran over to me.

I didn't answer him right away. A smile started to appear on my face. *Is it really?*

"Ash!"

I looked down at Jason, who was kneeling in front of me. His hands were on my knees and he looked scared as shit. I started to giggle. The flutters were still coming.

"Ash, please answer me!" he pleaded. "Are you okay?"

I giggled again. "I'm fine, Jason," I answered breathlessly.

"Will you please tell me what's the matter?" he frantically asked.

I didn't answer him. I did something better. I grabbed his hand and placed it on my stomach.

Jason scrunched his eyebrows together. I could tell he was confused and then his features changed.

"Oh my god!" Jason yelled. "Ash, is that what I think it is?"

Jason grabbed me by my upper arms and started to cry.

"Yeah, it is." I smiled. My eyes filled with tears. I couldn't believe this was happening.

Leaning his head down to my stomach Jason kissed it. "I love you so much, baby." Jason then looked up at me and smiled. "Me and your mommy love you so much."

***

Jason had late night classes every Tuesday and Thursday so I decided to make us a romantic dinner and surprise him. Of course I had to ask Jade for her help because my feet were just killing me so much from these little munchkins. After she helped me make Jason's favorite meal, spaghetti with garlic bread, I thanked her for all of her help and she went on home.

Setting the table, I poured us some ginger ale and waited for Jason to come home. Of course I only had to wait maybe five minutes and when he walked in, he dropped his backpack on the floor and looked over at me. "What's all this for?"

Getting up from the couch, I ran over to him and said, "I just wanted you to know how much I love you."

Kissing me on the lips, he said, "Thank you so much, baby." Kneeling down in front of me, he kissed my stomach. "How have you guys been for Mommy today?"

Giggling, I said, "Good for the most part. Although in the afternoon, they were bouncing all around. I swear I had to pee like fifty times."

"How are you doing today, Ashlynn?"

"Good. I talked to Dad and he said that he loved you and would see us soon." That made Jason smile. After kissing me again because he just couldn't resist, he took my hand in his and walked us over to the dinner table and helped me in my seat.

During dinner, Jason told me all about his classes and how he did all of his homework beforehand because he just wanted to spend the night with me. Looking at him, it still took my breath away. I don't think I would ever get over the fact that we took a chance and we came out on top. We made it through all of our messes; we finally made it to a place of happiness. A place of tranquility. A place filled with love.

Tilting his head, Jason asked, "What are you thinking about, Ash?"

"Just how everything has changed. This time last year we were getting ready to leave for Vegas. I just don't think I'll ever get over the fact that this is what I had in store for me. What we had in store for each other, and I can't even begin to imagine where we'll be next year. Six years from now. Twenty years from now. Jason, with you anything is possible. The word *impossible* doesn't exist in my vocabulary when it comes to you." Tears fell from my eyes.

Moving his chair back, Jason got up from his seat and walked over to me. Taking my hand in his, he pulled me up out of my seat and we walked back to our bedroom. Closing the door behind him, he turned to me and kissed me. I started to wrap my arms around his neck but he took my hands in his and lifted them up above my arms.

Placing his hands to the bottom of my shirt he pulled it up and over me. Biting his lower lip, he unclasped my bra and he let it fall to the floor, never taking his eyes off me. He then knelt down in front of me and pulled down my sweats and panties.

Looking up at me he said, "I love you so much, Ashlynn."

Standing up, he walked me backwards to the edge of his bed, but just before I was going to sit down, I placed a hand to his chest. He was breathing really heavily and I looked up at him and smiled. I undressed him as well, never taking my eyes off his. They were filled with such love and hunger and I started biting my lip.

I was about to get up from my knees but his cock was right in front of my face and my mouth instantly watered. Gripping him in my left hand while my right hand massaged his balls, I wet my lips and sucked the tip of him into my mouth. He put a hand in my hair to pull it away because I knew he loved watching me do this.

"Oh god, Ash," he moaned.

I took as much of him into my mouth without gagging as I could and began to bob my head up and down. A few bobs in, I knew Jason was close because he sucked in a breath and said my name. Even though I always swallowed, he always said my name before my mouth was filled with his cum.

Growing in my mouth, he stilled and squirted into my throat. I sucked everything he offered up to me and then wiped him clean with my tongue. Looking up at Jason, I licked my lips. Before I knew it, he was lifting me up onto the bed and kneeling in front of me. I could no longer lay on my back because it was too uncomfortable, so I had to sit up whenever he went down on me, which I didn't mind at all.

He first kissed my lips and then slowly moved down to my nipples. Sucking one into his mouth while he twisted the other, I got goose bumps all over. I was hypersensitive and aware of everything when Jason and I had sex while being pregnant. It just took every emotion and action to a whole new level.

I put my hands in his hair as he moved to give the other nipple the same attention. As soon as he sucked my nipple into his mouth, he pushed two fingers inside me. I gasped because I was just so head over heels, completely crazy in love with

Jason Williams. I felt the beginnings of an orgasm and as soon as he pushed another finger in, I went overboard. I fell off the cliff, but this time something felt wrong. It didn't feel right and I automatically knew why.

Releasing my nipple from his mouth and taking the three fingers out of me, Jason looked up at me. Barely whispering, he asked, "Ash?" I looked at him in pure amazement and let out a laugh.

We both knew what it was but I wanted to say it out loud. It didn't seem real until it left my lips. "Jason, my water just broke."

Chapter 18

Jason

I had just heard the most beautiful words come from Ash's lips. Putting her head in my hands and cradling her I asked, "Say it again, Ashlynn."

"My water just broke." Her eyes glistened with tears.

I felt tears forming in my eyes and before I knew it, salty liquid was falling from my face but I could not take my eyes off Ashlynn. She lifted her fingers to my face and started wiping them away but it was not even worth it.

Kissing her on the lips, I pulled away and said, "We're going to be parents."

Nodding with my hands on either side of her face, she said, "I know, Jason."

Laughing, I screamed, "We're going to be parents!"

Ashlynn just laughed at me and started to get up. But just when she started to push herself up off the bed, she put a hand to her stomach and bent over. "Jason we need to get going," she said. She grunted. "Like now!"

Quickly getting changed, I helped Ash back into her clothes, scooped her up, and carried her to the car. I buckled her in and then bolted back to the apartment and grabbed the overnight bag. To tell you the truth, I'm not even one hundred percent positive that I locked the door behind me because I was such a bundle of nerves. I tried to drive like a normal person but I was going crazy and Ash kept bending over and holding onto her stomach.

So I just said, "Fuck it," and slammed on the gas with my foot. We got to the hospital in less than ten minutes and thankfully a cop didn't pull me over for excessive speeding.

As soon as I parked, I jumped out of the car and ran over to Ash. She was opening the door and beginning to stand but I picked her up in my arms. Closing the door with my foot, I ran into the hospital as I heard Ash giggling and saying, "Calm down, Jason, everything is going to be fine."

Running into the hospital, I ran over to the receptionist's desk and said, "My girlfriend's water just broke. She's scheduled for a C-section next week." Lifting her eyes from the paper she was reading, the receptionist looked up and a huge smile grew on her face. Looking at Ash, I saw her lift her arms like she didn't know what the hell I was thinking.

The receptionist then returned eye contact with me and said, "Take a seat in the waiting room and I will call shortly."

I was just about to open my mouth when she put her hand up and said, "I'm just going to get a wheelchair for your girlfriend so we can take you guys back to the delivery room."

Shaking my head, I said, "It's fine—I'll carry her."

The receptionist turned to look at Ashlynn with a smile on her face. Giggling, she said, "Sir, I understand, but we need to put her in a wheelchair."

I frowned. "All right." Placing Ash down in the wheelchair, I kissed her on the forehead. Grabbing ahold of her hand, we went to the delivery room. It was overwhelming to think that in just a little while we would be parents.

I helped Ash onto the table looked into her eyes. "I love you so much, Ashlynn."

"I love you so much, Jason." Tears rolled down her cheeks.

Once Ashlynn changed into her nightgown and had the IV needle placed into her hand, she called her dad and told him that we were having the twins a week early. It was already eight in the evening and Garrett and Janie were four hours away, so Ashlynn said for them to not worry about it and that we would call if there was any news to break, no matter what time of night.

While Ash was on the phone with her dad, I called Jade and said, "Hey, Aunt Jade?"

I had to pull the phone away because she was screaming so loud and I started to laugh. "Well, you're not an aunt yet, but Ashlynn's water just broke and we're at the hospital."

Shrieking into the phone, she said, "Okay, Neil and I will be there soon," and hung up. After that we called Sarah and Gabe, Ryder and Isabelle, as well as Patrick and Derrick.

The second everyone arrived at the hospital, they ran in and greeted us. Jade was crying because she couldn't wait to hold the babies and spoil the hell out of them. Once everyone gave us their hugs and kisses, they went to the waiting room. As much as Ash wanted to give birth to the kiddos naturally, the doctor had opted against it when we found out we were having twins. I was fine with it, Ash on the other hand? Not so much. She wanted to give birth naturally.

I felt like such a jackass because I didn't know what to do. I didn't know the first thing about how to help her. I stood there as Ash changed into her gown and slippers. The nurse gave me a pair of scrubs to change into. My hands started to shake as I changed into them. I couldn't believe how nervous I was. To think I wasn't even giving birth to our children. I was so proud of Ashlynn. I knew she was strong willed, but this? I was proud to be her boyfriend and the father of her children.

Once we were all set, Ashlynn was wheeled into the OR. I held her hand the entire time, but I had to let go when she was moved onto the operating table. They placed a drape in front of her so Ash was unable to see.

Honestly? I didn't think I would be watching, either. As much as I wanted to see our children, I didn't want to see Ash's insides. So I opted against it. She completely understood.

"Okay," the anesthesiologist said. "I'm just going to give you an epidural. You will be awake for everything, which is the good part. The great part? You won't feel anything."

Ash nodded her head. "Okay," she whispered.

I knew she was nervous. I was scared as hell. Ash squeezed my hand and her eyes winced as she got the epidural.

"Okay. How are we doing?" the anesthesiologist asked.

Ash nodded. "I'm doing okay."

The door to the operating room then opened. "Okay," the doctor said, walking in. Along with him came another doctor, a surgical assistant, a few more nurses, as well as a neonatal nurse. "Are we ready to deliver these babies?"

"Yes," Ash said excitedly.

I didn't say anything. I started to feel a bit faint. I prepared for this for nine months, but I was starting to get nervous.

"Are you okay?" a nurse asked me as she placed a hand on my back.

I looked over towards her. "Yeah. Just nervous."

"I understand." Patting me on the back, she nodded her head towards Ash. "Why don't you hold her hand and keep her occupied?"

"Yeah. Thanks," I whispered. Leaning down next to Ash I whispered, "Hi, baby."

She looked up at me and smiled.

"I'm so proud of you, Ash," I whispered.

Ash just smiled at me.

I watched as tears fell from her eyes.

"Are you okay, baby?"

"Yeah," she whispered. "I just can't wait to see them."

I smiled. "Me too." I needed to touch Ash. Even though she was standing right in front of me, I needed to feel her skin against mine. I lifted my hand to move stray hairs from her face. Cupping her head in my hand, I smiled at her. *Who knew that just a simple touch from someone you loved deeply could calm you? Could be enough?*

The doctor said, "All right, it's time to have some babies."

"I'm so proud of you baby," I whispered into Ash's ear.

Tears rolled down her face.

"Does it hurt?" I asked, worried.

She giggled. "No, Jason. I just, I love you. So much."

I kissed her hand again and held it against my lips. "I love you too, baby."

"We have a boy," the doctor said.

I stood up and watched as he handed Bennett off to a nurse to get cleaned up.

"Is everything okay?" Ash asked.

I kneeled down again. "He's perfect, baby. They're just cleaning him up before we get to see him." Suddenly our son started to cry and we smiled at one another.

"And we have a girl," the doctor announced before handing Jaylin to a nurse.

I looked down at Ash. She was breathing heavily and tears were running down her face. I leaned over to her and kissed her on the forehead. "I love you so much, Ashlynn."

Running her hand along my face, she smiled. "I love you, Jason."

I couldn't believe they were finally here.

Jaylin and Bennett were taken out of the delivery room. Once Ash was sewn up, we went back into the hospital room. I stayed with her the entire time. I wanted to see our children, but I couldn't leave Ash's side. Plus she told me if I held the twins before her, she'd cut my balls off. The way she saw it, since she held Jaylin and Bennett for nine months, she deserved to hold them first. I was totally fine with it.

"How are you feeling, baby?" I asked as I rubbed her head.

"Good," she whispered. "How are they?"

"The nurse told me they're doing okay. We have a healthy baby boy and baby girl."

Ash gave me a small smile. "Good."

"I'm so proud of you Ash."

Ash smiled at me.

A few minutes later a nurse walked in. "How are we doing, Mom and Dad?"

Ash and I looked at one another with huge smiles on our faces. *Mom and Dad.*

"Good," Ash nodded. "Can we see our babies now?"

The nurse giggled. "Of course you can. I just want to make sure everything is okay with you first." Once the nurse checked Ash's vitals and temperature, we were taken into our hospital room.

As soon as Ash was all set up, the nurse said, "All right, I'll go get your babies for you."

Turning to me, Ash smiled. "I can't wait to see them," she said. She looked excited and tired all at the same time.

I let out a laugh. "Me neither."

"Here they are," the nurse said as she pulled one of the babies in, followed by another nurse with our other child.

Tears welled up in my eyes. I couldn't believe they were finally here. I sat down next to Ash on the bed. Our main nurse handed Ash our son while the other nurse handed me our daughter.

"They're beautiful." Ash smiled.

I couldn't take my eyes off our daughter. She was so beautiful, pure and innocent. I would do whatever it took to keep them children for as long as Ash and I could. I wouldn't let them grow up as fast as I had to.

***

"How are we all doing?" the nurse asked, walking back into the room.

"Good," Ash said.

The nurse smiled. "I'm Sally, by the way. How about we get those babies some food in them? You want to try it out, Ashlynn?"

Ash perked up. "Yes, please," she said happily. "And it's nice to meet you, Sally."

Sally smiled. "It's very nice to meet you too, Ashlynn. Jason," she said, looking over at me.

I just smiled.

Sally looked back over to Ashlynn. "Okay, sweetie. We're going to get you a pillow. This is how you'll feed your children. It's much easier this way for twins. May I have the little one?"

Ash pursed her lips. Clearly she didn't want to let go of Bennett.

Giggling, Sally said, "It will only be for a second."

Once Ash handed over Bennett to Sally, she placed him in his carrier. Placing a moon shaped pillow around Ash's waist, Sally said, "I promise you this will be a lot easier with feeding twins." Grabbing hold of Bennett, Sally handed him back to Ash.

Ash perked up and smiled.

Sally faced Bennett towards Ash. Turning to me, she sweetly asked, "Can I have her?"

Handing over Jaylin, Sally smiled. "Thank you." Setting Jaylin up the same way, Sally pulled Ash's robe down and started to get to work on feeding our children.

Ashlynn smiled. "Oh, this is so weird, but I love it."

For another half an hour, it was just the two of us and our son and daughter. We couldn't believe they were finally here.

"I love you, Ash."

Looking over at me, Ash smiled. "I love you, too."

Someone then knocked on the door. "Knock, knock," a familiar voice said.

"Hey, Jade," I said.

"Can we come in?" she asked hesitantly.

Ash giggled. "Yes! Come on in."

I walked over to Jade with Bennett in my arms. She looked down at him and cried even more. Lifting her hand to his face, she leaned in and kissed him.

Jade looked up at me and said, "I'm so happy for you two." With an arm still holding Bennett, I lifted my other over Jade's arm and pulled her in for a hug. *I don't think my sister will ever have a clue just how much I love her and what lengths I would go to protect her.*

Looking back over at Ashlynn, I noticed she had tears in her eyes and was smiling at the both of us.

Walking over with Bennett in my arms, I sat down on the hospital bed and kissed Ashlynn. When, "I love you, Ashlynn," left my mouth, I turned my head down and looked at baby Jaylin. Jade sat down on the other side of me and just looked in awe at both of mine and Ashlynn's children.

I was still so numb from the experience that I almost didn't hear the nurse ask, "So what are these little ones' names?"

I looked over at Ashlynn and nudged my head for her to tell the nurse. Smiling at me she looked down at our daughter and said, "Jaylin Annabelle Williams."

As I kissed her on the forehead, she turned to our son and said, "Bennett Lee Williams."

Once the nurse got our information and left, we heard Sarah say, "I don't hear screaming anymore."

That's when Jade looked at us in question and at the same time, we both said, "Go get them."

Smiling, she jumped off the bed and ran out the door.

Seconds later, everyone came walking in with smiles on their faces and tears in their eyes.

Choking up, I said, "Ashlynn and I would like to introduce you to our daughter, Jaylin Annabelle Williams, and our son, Bennett Lee Williams." For about a half hour we passed our children around to everyone and explained how we came up with the names.

Gabe had Sarah wrapped up in arms, Ryder was holding Isabelle's hand, and then I noticed Neil smiling at Jade while she held Bennett in her arms. Ashlynn must have noticed because she wrapped her hand in mine and mouthed, "Not now." Shaking my head, I then saw Derrick kiss Patrick on the cheek and my mouth dropped open. *What the fuck was going on?*

Everybody must have noticed my mouth drop because the room went quiet except for the little noises coming from our children. That's when Derrick looked over at me and then to Ash, and started laughing. He bent over and rested his hands on his knees and laughed, "You never told him, did you?"

What the fuck was he talking about?

I looked around at everyone in the room and they had these faces like they were trying not to laugh and then I made my way over to Ash. She was biting her lip.

Sitting down on the bed, I said, "You want to explain something to me?"

Clearing her throat, she pointed to Derrick and said, "We kind of fake dated. Derrick's gay and he was dealing with some problems and I kind of vented about how I wanted to make you jealous …"

With wide eyes, I said, "Go on."

Gulping, she said, "So we fake dated. Derrick wasn't dealing with bullies questioning his sexuality anymore and, um, well, you know the rest." She bent her head out of shame and I just started laughing.

Placing a hand to the bottom of her chin, I lifted it up so she would look in my eyes. Smiling, I said, "You better start picking out another name for a little one, because the second you're better I'm getting you pregnant again." After I kissed her on the lips, I got up and walked over to Derrick. Placing a hand out in front of him, I said, "I'm sorry for acting like such a prick towards you."

He looked down at my hand then pulled me into a hug. "All's good, man. I knew you had it bad for my girl over there."

After I walked back over to Ashlynn's side, I couldn't help but look over at Derrick and Patrick and smile. I kind of felt like an idiot because anyone could see just how much they loved each other. I was too blindsided by the "dating" aspect that I didn't see the real picture right in front of me.

Once everyone got to hold both babies, they gave us each a hug and kiss and left to go home. Sitting there holding Jaylin while Ashlynn held Bennett, I pulled out my cell phone and made a quick call. I knew it was late, but I wanted to give them the good news. I few rings in I heard, "H - hello?"

Through a smile, I said, "Hey, Grandpa," and then I heard the phone drop.

Pulling away from me, I put it on speaker and heard, "What did you say, Jason?"

"I said, 'Hey, Grandpa.'"

"You guys had the babies already?"

Looking over to Ash, she cried and said, "You are the grandpa to Jaylin Annabelle and Bennett Lee Williams." I then heard Garrett choke and begin to cry. Ash told him all about the delivery and said that I was amazing throughout the whole process. I looked over to her and half smiled and teared up. *If I was amazing, then Ashlynn was fucking fantastic, amazing, phenomenal.*

I said, "Night, Grandpa," and through laughter, Garrett said, "Night, Mom and Dad."

Shutting the phone off and placing it in my pocket, I looked down at Bennett and Jaylin.

We sat there for a few minutes in silence, kissing and hugging our son and daughter but then Ashlynn jumped and said, "Oh my god."

I didn't want to take my eyes away from my daughter but I did and looked over at her beautiful mother. She was looking at me and then just started to cry. Lifting a hand to wipe away the tears, I asked, "What's the matter, Ashlynn?"

Wiping away her tears with one hand, with Bennett in the other, she swallowed and said, "Jaylin and Bennett were born on March 12th."

Nodding my head, I said, "Um, yeah, and your point is?"

Ash just laughed. "Don't you see?"

Shaking my head back and forth, I said, "Apparently not. What's the significance of March 12th?"

Choking through her words, Ashlynn said, "The number 312. Jason, 312 was the number of mine and Jade's room freshman year of college. It was the hospital room number where your father passed away, and it was the day my mom was born."

Taking my eyes away from Ash, I looked between our daughter Jaylin and our son Bennett and just cried. Looking over at Ash, I said, "If I didn't think miracles existed before this, I definitely know they do now."

Smiling at me, she said, "I knew miracles existed the second I met you."

Closing my eyes, I felt tears streaming down my face, and opening them, Ash was smiling at me. Taking ahold of my hand, she asked, "Why are you crying, Jason?"

Shaking my head back forth, I said, "I don't believe that a mess like me ended up with a life that's so beautiful."

Taking my hand to her lips and kissing it she said, "Well, believe it."

Emily McKee

Epilogue

2 months later

Jason

It was finally here. Today Sarah, Gabe, Isabelle, Ryder, Jade, Derrick, Ashlynn, and I were graduating from college. Garrett and Janie met us at the stadium, where they held Jaylin and Bennett as their mom and dad walked across the stage and got their diplomas. I just could not believe the whirlwind roller coaster Ashlynn and I had been on this past year and how far we've come.

Sitting in the back of the student class with Jade by my side, I had a perfect view of Ashlynn as she sat and waited for her name to be called. One by one we were each called up to receive our diplomas. Derrick with a major in Education. Isabelle majored in Journalism. Gabe with a major in Mathematics and Sarah received a Nursing major. Ryder did a double major in Business and Marketing. Jade with a double major in Chemistry and Biology, *yeah, I know my sister is fucking smart*. Ash majored in Art Therapy and I graduated with a major in Biochemical Engineering.

Once we received our diplomas and threw our caps in the air, I ran over to Ashlynn. Wrapping her arms around me as I picked her up by the waist, our lips met. I could never get enough of having her lips on mine. She started to swipe along my bottom lip and I could not help growling.

Smiling against my mouth, she said, "I love you, Jason."

Placing her back down on the ground, I said, "I love you, Ashlynn."

Releasing her arms from around my neck, she took my hand in hers and we started to search out Garrett and Janie because we just couldn't wait to see Jaylin and Bennett. That last two months of school were pretty difficult on the both of us. We barely got any sleep as we took care of our children yet somehow we graduated with High Honors.

How we did that I will never know.

We spotted Garrett and Janie and were on our way over when I saw Jade wrap her arms around Neil and he kissed her on the neck. I instantly fumed and started to walk over in that direction but Ashlynn pulled me along with her and said, "Leave them be, Jason. Your sister looks happy." I was glad my sister was happy but Neil made me a promise and he broke it. Big fucking mistake on his part because I would be watching him.

Reaching Garrett and Janie, I grabbed Jay while Ash grabbed Bennett. Kissing each of our kids on the foreheads, Garrett and Janie then gave us a hug and kiss each and said, "Congratulations, you guys."

Ash then handed Bennett over to me and wrapped her arms around her dad. He kissed her on the cheek and hugged her while he said, "I'm so proud of you, baby."

Through tears, she said, "I love you so much, Dad." Letting go of Ash, he then walked up to me.

I handed Jay and Ben to Ash and then Garrett hugged me and said, "I'm so proud of you, son."

Through tears, I wrapped my arms around his middle and said, "Thanks so much, for everything."

Leaning away from me, he smiled and patted me on the back. Taking Bennett, I handed him to Janie and said, "Ash, do you mind giving Jay to your dad?"

With this weird look on her face, she nodded and said, "Okay." Handing Jay to her dad, she then turned around to see me on my knee in front of her holding out a ring box.

Opening the ring box, I said, "I told you someday that I would tell you the conversation your dad and I had the first time we talked on the phone the night before Sarah and Gabe's wedding."

Looking at Garrett, who had tears in his eyes, I smiled and then looked back at Ashlynn. "Well, I asked him for his permission to marry you. I fought my feelings for you so much over the years because I didn't want to drag you into my mess. I didn't want to damage your beauty, but I broke the rules and I fell in love with you, Ashlynn Miller.

"Will you marry me?"

Falling to her knees and wrapping her arms around me, she said, "Yes, Jason! Yes!"

I wrapped my arms around her and just held on for dear life. I was never going to let this girl go. Standing up, I placed the ring on her finger and kissed her. I heard cheers from our friends and even people we didn't know.

Looking down at the ring, she said, "I can't believe this."

Rubbing my thumb across her cheek, I said, "Believe it."

After getting congratulations from everybody, Garrett and Janie handed us back our kids. I had an arm wrapped around Ash as I looked down at her and she looked up at me and then we saw a flash go off. We looked over and saw Jade had taken a picture of us. Wiping her eyes, she said, "You guys just looked so beautiful."

Smiling, I looked back at Ashlynn, Jaylin, and Bennett. For the life of me, I couldn't get the huge smile off my face because I never thought I would be here. I never thought on the drive up to school my freshman year of college that my life would change so drastically. I never thought I would meet a girl who would completely change my world and make me question everything. I never thought in a million years I would ever find it in my heart to forgive my dad or fall in love with my best friend. I never thought I could have what I have right now: my soon-to-be wife, our son Bennett, and our daughter Jaylin … a family.

Ashlynn once told me that she was the beautiful to my mess and even to this day that still stands.

Through the hardships and the struggles, through the love and the laughter, together Ashlynn and I made a beautiful mess.

The End

Acknowledgements

I have to first start off by saying thank you to all of the readers. I am truly humbled and grateful by this rollercoaster of a life I now have. I feel like I'm on Cloud 9 or that I'm asleep and having the best dream ever. If so, I never want to wake up.

Mom & Jared, thank you for the support and words of encouragement you both have given me in pursuing my dream.

Josh, words can't describe just how grateful I am to have you in my life. You are my kissy monster, my cheerleader, my cuddle buddy ... my best friend. You mean everything to me and I don't know if this experience would be the same for me if you weren't here to share it with. I love you so much.

Alessandra, thank you for helping me through this fun yet difficult process. I don't think you have any idea how much easier you have made it for me.

Thank you to Limitless Publishing for taking a huge chance on me. Jennifer O' Neill and Jessica Gunhammer, much thanks!

Toni Rakestraw for editing, Robin Harper of *Wicked by Design,* for the beautiful covers, Dixie Matthews for formatting, and Olivia Osland for your amazing marketing skills. Thank you all so much!

And last, but certainly not least, to everyone who has read my books. Thank you for making my dream a reality. I am so humbled by this life-changing experience and I have all of you to thank for it. I'm truly astonished by this writing process and I am at a loss for words to describe just how grateful I am for all of you, which is funny because I write books now!

XoXo, Emily!

About the Author

For the past 21 years, I have been a planner and an organizer. I always needed things a specific way and then everything changed for me. I've always had a vivid imagination and thoughts racing through my mind. I realized that life is way too short to let things pass me by, because in the blink of an eye everything could change. So I decided to just live in the moment, taking every chance and opportunity led my way. No second thoughts and just living in the moment.

I decided to put the fictional characters and the conversations going on in my head to paper. I know, it makes me sound crazy, but I wouldn't have it any other way. I've embraced crazy and hectic and last minute because it's led me to making my dreams a reality.

When I'm not writing Happily Ever Afters I'm reading about them and living one. I think this world is filled with too much sadness already we don't need to read about it as well. I write because I love it and I've allowed my imagination to run wild and be crazy and free. Just like me.

Contact Emily

Facebook:
www.facebook.com/pages/Emily-McKee/1411551212390451

Twitter:
@EmilyMcKee1206

Goodreads:
www.goodreads.com/author/show/7079840.Emily_McKee

Amazon:
www.amazon.com/Emily-McKee/e/B00DE3QVGW

Made in the
USA
Monee, IL